VERUM MALUM

Michael R. Collins

Uncomfortably Dark Horror

Contents

POST-RITUM

THE RITUAL HAD ENDED. Something ticked in the back of the dim room. It could be the wood and plaster responding to the energy they had raised. It could be something tapping its claws against bones. It could be completely imagined. The circle of people would believe any of these things readily. A body lay in the middle of the room, its torso opened and empty, entrails scattered about. A large hexagram filled with symbols and sigils lay under the blood.

At the head sat an older man, his black robe open, his shirt underneath soaked and sticking to his pudgy body. His breath heavy as he pulled the cowl back. What little hair he had was plastered to his head with sweat. To his left lay a young man, still as death.

Going around the points of the hexagram, each of the others came to their senses. A blond teen shook his head and then spat a bloody gob of kidney onto the floor. Beside him, another man, this one only a few years older, found his shaky legs and stood. Naked but for his boxers, he scanned the room and searched the corners left dark from the dying candlelight. He slicked

5

his brown hair back with sticky hands. A woman who lay near the eviscerated body stretched and sat up. Naked, her torso was covered in blood, her hands and mouth dripping with it.

"What have we done?" a hoarse voice asked.

They all turned toward the speaker.

A man stood at the only door to the room, taking in the horror before him. "We've debased ourselves, we've killed, and we've introduced an evil into our world."

"I thought that was the point," the older man said, covering himself with his robe. He found his legs and stood. "You knew what the end result was to be. This should come as no surprise."

"By calling on that demon, you've led us all straight to Hell, Alexander," the man accused.

"And we will go together, happily led by the work we've accomplished here. Ben, it's too late to run away."

"Watch me," Ben said, his hand on the door handle.

"You won't get far. If 'Hell' won't be on your heels, you know we will," the brown-haired man said. His piercing stare forced Ben to look away.

"If I ever see you again, Marius, you can count your days on one hand." Ben opened the door and slipped through.

They heard his bare feet slap against the steps.

"What are we going to do about him?" the woman asked, her voice thick and sluggish.

"Don't worry about him, Scarlet. We have done a glorious thing. Let him go for now. Ben will get what is coming to him. I will make sure of it." Alexander looked at the others. "I'm afraid Jacob didn't make it." The prone body still did not move. "Parker, I trust you will want to tend to your cousin."

The blond teen stared at the body. He nodded after a moment.

As the others continued to collect themselves, only Marius seemed unaffected, his hawkish gaze studying his companions with increasing intensity.

I

Five Years Later

NOAH SAT ON THE couch, staring at the phone in his hands. The thick silence of the living room unnerved him. He realized it wasn't the room that had become quiet but his own head. It came from shock, not surprise. A throbbing numbness yielded to sharp anger. He remembered from experience the coming emotions: betrayal, sorrow, rage, and loss. That, however, didn't mean he would be prepared for them.

He gently put the phone down, afraid of awakening it. If he did, it might have more bad news, worse than what he had just received. If that was possible. He walked across the room to the small, expensive stereo and flicked it on. Loud syrupy pop music blared from the speakers. He turned it down enough to just make out the tiny thump of percussion and buzz of vocals. Noah didn't want the music, but he couldn't stand the silence.

He stood in the kitchen, staring at the refrigerator. He didn't even know why he went in there aside from the momentary distraction of movement. The cupboard above the cheap Frigidaire held an even better distraction. Opening the cupboard, he removed a bottle of vodka. Behind it sat a half-finished bottle of Southern Comfort.

He held the vodka in one hand, the Southern Comfort in the other. He put the vodka back. Noah didn't care for the clear liquor—it tasted like cleaner to him. Despite an insistent voice in his head telling him to cease and desist, he filled a glass tumbler with ice. Each cube cracked and popped in its turn as he poured the dark amber liquid over it. The voice in his head became louder, warning him. Noah knew the voice in his head was Ben's, and he found it easier to ignore than expected.

Ben smelled the alcohol before seeing the glass on the living room table. Their small house, decorated in dark art deco, could hide few secrets. The glass was mostly empty. Only a few melting ice cubes remained.

"Noah?" Ben called out as he shrugged off his hoodie.

"Welcome home, dear," came a caustic reply from the kitchen. Noah emerged, his eyes red, his tawny cheeks flushed. "How was your day?"

Ben could tell that Noah hadn't completely passed over the threshold of drunkenness but had one toe over the line. Off the wagon after doing so well, he lamented.

"I should ask you the same thing," he said, maintaining a friendly tone. "I see you've been relaxing."

'Relaxing' had been a term they used years ago when he would often find Noah drunk, a bottle nearby.

"Come relax with me." Fumes of rage followed Noah as he stomped to the couch and flopped down on it. "Have a drink." He patted the space beside him.

"We should have thrown that bottle out," Ben sighed, sitting on the edge of the cushion next to his husband. "What's this about?"

"We should have a toast. It's a good day for toasts, don't you agree?" Noah sprang back up. "I'll get you a drink, and we'll toast."

"What are we going to toast to?" Ben asked, knowing he shouldn't enable Noah's behavior.

"Your fucking health, that's what!" Noah shouted.

Ben said nothing. He stared at his shoes and ran his hand through his short dark hair.

Noah stood there, staring at him, waiting for him to look up again.

"I take it the doctor called? I haven't even gotten the results back yet. How did you?" Ben asked, making eye contact again.

"He called earlier today," Noah said, his voice lower but no less angry.

"He had no right to tell you. That was between him and me," Ben countered half-heartedly. This was not a fight he would win. Nor did he want to.

"Since your oncologist is my uncle, it would've been hard to keep it a secret for long. How long did you think you'd hide the fact that you were no longer in remission? Did you think I wouldn't notice?" Noah's eyes grew red and moist, and Ben had to turn away. He had seen those eyes like that too often in the past.

"It was just a routine check. No one suspected a thing. After the last time, we were so sure we beat the cancer. I didn't expect it to come back."

"I understand that, I guess." Noah's tone grew softer as his ire subsided. "Is there anything else you want to tell me?"

Ben cursed Dr. Anderson, Uncle Teddy, for being so forthcoming with his nephew. "There is no point going in for treatment. If it's coming back too aggressive, all it would do is delay the inevitable."

"Bullshit, Ben. We still have a chance if it is treated hard and fast. Do it now," Noah exploded again. His dark face, normally pleasant and animated, twisted in forms of sorrow and rage. "You said last time that—"

"I'm not going through it again," Ben finished for him. "It's back for a reason, and I would rather let it run its course. If cancer is the way I go, then I accept it."

"I can't accept it!"

"You're not the one dying," Ben said in a flat tone.

With that, Noah deflated and sat back on the couch. He laid his head on the broad shoulder of his husband.

"I know, and you're right—I'm not the one dying. It feels like it, though." He looked up at Ben's face, at his strong chin and prominent nose. Along an olive-colored cheek was a small shallow scar for which Ben always had a new story. That face, he would have to memorize its eastern Mediterranean lines again. He would have to take it all in, like the last time, before the chemo and radiation ravaged him.

They talked the rest of the evening. While Ben cooked, and then after dinner, they worked it out. After dessert they made love passionately and with purpose. Then they did it again, for no other reason than they could. Noah fell asleep right after, but Ben lay awake. He watched Noah sleep, his handsome face at peace, and played with an errant hair, dark brown in the night's shadow, until he snuffled and turned over.

He would call the doctor in the morning even though he didn't feel any different. If the cancer had come back and he felt nothing, maybe it was still treatable. He hoped so, for Noah's sake. For his own sake, maybe letting it run its course would be the best thing. If that were the case, at last, he could admit he had outrun the Devil long enough.

II

ALEXANDER SAT, WEARING ONLY a t-shirt and silk black robe. In front of him lay a spread of cards. He had commissioned the art of this tarot deck, each hand-painted to his explicit instructions. They depicted gruesome scenes in strokes of vivid colors. From the downturned deck he flipped over a card with dry pudgy fingers. On the front of the card hung a person, neither male nor female, a rope strung around their broken neck. They hung from a gothic-style cross. At its base, a smudged pile of shit and piss.

Alexander set the worn card into place and flipped another. Its face bore the image of a small child impaled by five swords against a brick wall. He placed it down and sighed, interpreting the spread. Across from him sat Marius, bored but not uninterested.

"Well, what do the cards say?" Marius' knowledge and trust in the occult and supernatural rivaled that of Alexander's. He had known the man for years and mined all the information possible from him. Of all the practices in the dark arts, the tarot remained the one thing he still reserved his doubts about. Soothsaying stretched his beliefs a bit far. Now, unless the cards were being guided by another force, something more demonic, that would be different.

"They say we are on the right track," Alexander whispered. He stared at the cards for a few moments longer, swiped them up, and shuffled them back into the deck. "We are on the right track, but our goal will not be easy to obtain. There will be death."

"That goes without saying. We can't finish what we started without some death," Marius said, standing up and letting the blood flow back into his legs. "To be honest, I'm counting on a little death."

"I mean death for us. We might lose a few in the process. All great things come with sacrifice. And I don't mean those we offer up as sacrifices. We must proceed with caution from here on out. We must calculate each move we make."

Alexander stood and placed the cards back into a black velvet pouch. Marius looked away as he did. He had never been squeamish with nudity, but he grew tired of seeing Alexander's flaccid penis. The man seemed to abhor pants.

"Are you saying that little phone call we made yesterday might have been foolish?" Marius leaned against a nearby wingback chair. It creaked under his weight. He played with the tattered seams.

"No. Causing some chaos here and there is fun, and it has its purpose. Ben is smart, cowardly, but smart. I'm sure this will disrupt his life and stir things up. But it won't take him long to figure out what our game is." Alexander closed his robe and made his way into the kitchen.

"Are you sure we need him? If he was a weak link once, he will be so again," Marius called after him.

"We need him. His energies are too intertwined with our work. We've gone as far as we can without him." Alexander's voice echoed from the kitchen.

The old house had belonged to his family for generations. The group had moved in after Alexander's widowed aunt died a year ago. While Marius enjoyed plotting devious schemes in an old Victorian home, he wished it didn't belong to his mentor. Despite the perfect mood it provided for their work, he bristled at anything related to Alexander. Even the very sight of him turned his stomach. If the older man wanted to talk about weaker links, Marius decided the weakest link wasn't Ben but Alexander.

As Alexander grubbed around the kitchen, Marius sat again and turned over ideas in his head. The whole point of summoning the demon five years ago involved gaining knowledge and power. But his companions were too shortsighted. They didn't want the power the demon could bestow; they just wanted to bask in the presence of it. He wanted more. The demon only represented one step toward the eventual goal: contact the ultimate evil. To negotiate power with the True Evil, to glimpse its domain of torture and damned souls—that was the end result. Marius had big plans. He now realized that Alexander had been talking a much bigger game than he could offer, and that simply wouldn't do.

"I've mined all the information I can from him," Marius muttered. "He'll have to go soon."

He would still have Parker and Scarlet. Conspiring with them against Alexander would do no good; they had no loyalty. They only wanted to follow whoever possessed the power to bring about the ultimate evil. They were driven by results. Why else would they have stayed on after the debacle with the demon? Another idea occurred to him as Alexander walked back in holding a dripping sandwich. Mayo and mustard oozed and commingled on his fingers, making it look like ejaculate on his hand. Again, his robe had come open. Marius shuddered in revulsion.

"You're right about Ben. He should rejoin us. He's marked like us. It'll make it easier. Plus, he will make a fine sacrifice. One less dark-skinned coward on the planet." Marius forced a smile.

Alexander, mouth full of sandwich, nodded in agreement. "Even better," he said around his food, breadcrumbs and a chunk of cheese falling from the corner of his mouth. "He needs a reminder of who is in charge. Once Ben realizes we are back in his life, we'll get all our preparations finalized. Parker and Scarlet need something to do; they are getting too restless and sloppy. That mess they made in the church last night was pure carelessness."

Marius said nothing. He nodded and left the sitting room. Parker and Scarlet's sprees, and their taste for madness and blood, meant nothing to him. He would give them something to occupy their time soon enough. Something more than desecrating churches out of boredom.

He passed by the empty dining room, the windows covered up with brown paper and speckled with paint here and there. From the outside, it gave the illusion of repairs being done, but really, they used the space for rituals. Up the squeaking stairs, he climbed to his drafty bedroom. He would spend the night reading over the forbidden books again, staving off restlessness. If he could perform the work without the others, he would have already. Over the years, he had grown to hate them. If things went in his favor, they would all be his sacrifices to the Ultimate Evil. Alexander being the first.

As he reached the top of the stairs, he saw Scarlet hovering around Parker's bedroom door. She listened to the noises that came from behind it. Scarlet, her hair over-dyed with red, dressed in her usual array of ratty fishnets and leather. She smelled as if she had come from a local punk show: stale cigarettes, amphetamines, and angry horniness. Good chance she went to see Emaciated Angel, Marius mused. They were a death metal band whose members had been led to believe Marius and Alexander would teach them their 'evil ways.' Instead, Alexander used them as a source of extra cash.

"You think Parker knows that Jacob isn't real?" Scarlet whispered, her ear still to the door. "I mean, he was there when Jacob died during the ritual. But the way he talks to thin air…"

"He is aware," Marius answered, pausing. "He is also aware that his hallucinations are only that. I don't think he cares. But it's not Jacob he's in there talking to. He brought home some waitress. I'm sure by now she's drugged and used to his satisfaction."

"Scarlet, I know you're there," Parker called from the other side of the door. "You can have her now if you want!"

"Ah, right on cue," Marius mumbled as she opened the door.

"Oh, she's cute." Scarlet pulled a long, thin stiletto knife from the pocket of her patched leather vest and entered the room. "At least she's still alive. I can have a little fun still. You need to bring home a guy one of these days. I get horny, too."

"I don't do guys," Parker reminded her as she closed the door behind her.

Marius disappeared into his room, hoping they wouldn't get too loud.

III

"DO YOU REMEMBER WHO you talked to?" Dr. Ted Anderson's voice blared from Ben's phone. It sat on the cushion between Ben and Noah. They loomed over the device, catching every syllable. Ben unconsciously rolled the bottom hem of his untucked shirt between his fingers.

"I swore it was you, Uncle Teddy. I mean, it sounded just like you. Is there another oncologist that sounds like you that might have called instead?" Noah said into the phone. He held relief at arm's length, not trusting it yet.

"The only other one is Dr. Bennett, and her voice is way prettier than mine. Listen, boys, I'm looking at the test results right now. In fact, I didn't even get them until this morning. Ben, you are clean. The cancer is still in remission, and everything else looks good. I don't know who would have called you, but it was a damned rotten thing to do. Maybe someone tried playing a bad joke on you?"

"A real bad joke," Ben muttered.

"Noah, I'd find the person who called you and kick their ass. Doesn't your mom still have some cousins in Cuba who practice Santeria? All I'm saying is—"

"I'm going to stop you right there, Uncle Teddy. Let's concentrate on Ben."

"Sorry, you're right."

Noah loved his uncle, but he was from his dad's side of the family. White and a little clueless.

"As far as I can see," Teddy continued, "everything is good. Seems someone wanted to cause trouble."

They heard both fear and anger in Uncle Teddy's voice. Despite it all, he remained one of the few in Noah's family, other than his parents, who supported him unconditionally when he came out. They had been close ever since.

"Oh, I plan on figuring this out," Noah said. "Listen, we'll stop in tomorrow to officially look at the test results."

His uncle agreed, and they said goodbye.

Ben looked at Noah. They both sighed. Noah's eyes grew moist. Ben hugged him close. "False alarm. Things are okay. It was only a false alarm."

They sat there, intertwined for some time, enjoying the good news they had received. Ben eventually disengaged and stood up. "Let's call Jackie and a few others, have a get-together tonight. Celebrate the fact that I still don't have cancer."

"I'd like to forget the whole thing," Noah sighed.

"We don't have to tell them why we're celebrating. It'll be nice to be with friends right now. We've both been a little too cooped-up lately."

"I can't argue with that. And if you want to rip into me about yesterday, go ahead. I deserve it." Noah winced at his weakness with the bottle.

Ben looked at him and their eyes locked. If Ben had a superpower, it was this. Noah had no escape, nor could he lie when Ben had him like this. "As long as you're good, we can forget it. If you need a meeting, we'll go now."

Noah shook his head. "What we need to do is find out who made that phone call. Who would get off lying to us like that? It's beyond cruel. We can't have pissed anyone off so bad as to do something that evil, could we?"

A dark look passed over Ben's face before he responded. "Maybe it was a prank, someone who wanted to cause some random trouble."

He tried to play it off, but Noah wasn't buying it.

"You know something." Noah gave him a severe look.

"I know lots of things. I know when I get my hands on the person who made that phone call, there will be the Devil to pay."

NOAH SWORE UNDER HIS breath. People were going to show up at any moment, and of all things, they had forgotten to buy wine. Jackie would have her fair share and Layne was a two-glass minimum.

He placed the covered relish tray in the refrigerator, minus the carrot he had stolen. Ben cycled through music in the living room, trying to find something soothing and dinner-partyish. For a moment, he heard the churning of shredding guitars and the kinetic barrage of double bass drums. Noah peered out of the kitchen as Ben looked over and gave him a grin. Noah rolled his eyes in mock exasperation and shook his head, unable to hide his own grin.

The Emaciated Angel album for which Noah had done the artwork would often find its way into random playlists. A little joke they liked to play on each other.

Noah wasn't much for it, but Ben had listened to it a few times. His musical tastes had always been a little rougher around the edges than his own. The tinkling piano of smooth jazz wafted into the kitchen, something neither of them cared for, but it sufficed for decent background music.

"We have no wine," Noah said after crunching his way through the purloined carrot.

"I did that on purpose." He gave his husband a knowing look. "You had a backslide. Our guests can live without it."

"Don't let our guests suffer because I'm weak. Go get some. I don't even like wine; it gives me a headache." Noah pointed at his head with the remainder of the orange vegetable. "Especially if you get a red."

"Nope. No wine, liquor, or beer. You've been doing so well. I don't want to ruin it with one slip. This week was enough." Ben took him in a big hug and kissed him on the forehead. "I don't want anything to happen to you. We're strictly prohibition now."

Noah melted into Ben's arms, hoping the love surrounding him right now would overpower the guilt. "So, if we're in prohibition, what's the password to get into your speakeasy?"

Laughing, Ben pushed him away.

"What? We should have time."

"You are incorrigible. Jackie will show up just as we get started. It's like she has a sixth sense about it. By the way, Carrie said she's bringing a friend. Apparently, she met this guy at a coffee shop. Claims to know one of us," Ben said as he moved into the living room to turn the music down a little more.

"Which one of us?" Noah followed him, catching sight of Jackie through the front window as she attempted to parallel park.

"No idea. She didn't say. And be nice to Layne this time. They have been going through a rough time."

"I'm always nice to Layne. We had one lively discussion about Goya, that's it."

"You accused them of having no taste in classic art." Ben raised an eyebrow.

"To be fair, who doesn't like Goya?"

"People who don't make a living creating creepy horror book illustrations and painting album covers for metal bands."

Jackie breezed through the house like she owned it. Being Noah's best friend for so long had earned her the right. Fiercely protective of Noah and Ben, she considered them her boys, and God help anyone who messed with them.

"Gentlemen, the party has arrived." She gave an exaggerated curtsy, handed Noah a plate of cold cuts, and gave Ben a peck on each cheek. She took the plate back from Noah and disappeared into the kitchen.

THE EVENING STARTED WELL. Jackie, in her pencil skirt, waistcoat, ruffled blouse, and bat print bow tie, answered the door for each guest while insisting the boys relax. Noah knew she sensed the recent tensions. It was a small get-together, and all but one of their friends had shown up. Bryce and Layne, college friends of Noah's, took turns with Jackie's time. Patrick and Marcello peppered Ben with medical questions, as their dear friend had been recently diagnosed with pancreatic cancer.

Noah wasn't happy with the subject, but Ben handled it with aplomb. Tangela sat on the couch enjoying the music and filling Noah in on all the juicy gossip since reconnecting with her family. They had struggled with her gender transition but were at least trying to understand it.

The doorbell rang.

Jackie called out, "I'll get it."

She had been glassy-eyed for fifteen minutes over Bryce's detailed description of the interdepartmental politics at the university. She opened the door to see Carrie, a slight woman in her mid-forties who wore a gray wool coat rain or shine. Next to her stood a tall man with intense eyes. His features were sharp and precise. A smile spread across his face, and it made Jackie uneasy. It was an attempt at friendly warmth, and it failed. Something about this man made her want to block his way in. He shouldn't be here.

Despite her split-second reluctance, she stepped back. Before she could utter a hello, Ben came rushing out from the back of the room.

"What the fuck are you doing here?"

With a yelp, Jackie jumped out of the way.

All the color drained from Carrie's face.

The tall stranger stood there with a fake smile still plastered on his face.

"You need to leave right fucking now!"

Everyone stood shocked, staring at Ben. He did not raise his voice in anger often, and never like this. Waves of hate radiated from him.

"How the hell did you find me, Marius?" Ben stood toe to toe with him. "Why are you here?"

"It's not like you are hard to find. Especially when you are married to someone so talented." Marius glanced over Ben's shoulder at Noah.

Noah said nothing, not wanting to ignite anything further. He had seen Ben's anger before. It was hot and blistering and scared the hell out of him. Jackie sensed it, too, and took hold of Carrie, dragging the petrified woman some distance into the house and away from the two.

"I will say this only once," Ben snarled. "Get the hell away from me, my husband, my house, my everything. If I ever see you again, I'll send you straight to Hell."

Marius didn't budge. "Isn't that where we planned to meet, anyway?" He took a half-step back and gave a slight nod of the head. "I don't wish to linger where I am not welcome, so I will go. Thank you for bringing me along, Carrie, but it seems I must leave. Ben will explain why." He turned and walked away. As he did, he called out, "The others say hello, Ben. Shall I send your regards to them?"

Ben slammed the door.

Noah took long strides across the room to his husband as the others remained still.

His face still twisted by rage, Ben turned away from the door. Carrie clung to Jackie as Ben's gaze fell on her. Seeing her confusion and fear, his anger deflated as he realized the scene he had just made.

"I'm so sorry, Carrie," he quickly apologized. "He's someone from a long time ago, someone I hoped to never see again. You had no way of knowing our history. Promise me you will have nothing to do with him. He's a dangerous person. A *very* dangerous person."

Carrie tried to say something, the intensity of the moment making it difficult to focus until she blurted out the first thing that came to mind: "But he was my ride!"

THE PARTY DIDN'T LAST as long as Ben and Noah hoped. But after the altercation, an awkward air hung thickly over the event, so they saw its end as a mercy. Only Jackie stayed afterward to help clean. Noah put the half-eaten veggie tray back in the fridge while Jackie appreciated a painting Noah had been working on. Ben sat on the couch, a bottle of water in hand, his thoughts a million miles away.

"I am going to Hell," Ben said à propos to nothing.

Jackie turned away from the painting of a ghoulish face only half colored.

Noah came in from the kitchen, already shaking his head. "Let's not start this up again."

"Yes, this again. You need to listen this time. No more ignoring me." Ben took another drink of water. "I'm serious."

"I don't believe in the whole 'heaven-hell' thing. Satan is not waiting for you. No God has judged you evil." Noah seated himself across from Ben and took his hand. "You are an amazing man, and there is no way you are going to Hell just because you kicked some guy off of our doorstep."

Jackie said nothing. Noah had talked to her about Ben's insistence that he was going to Hell. She remembered that neither of them was particularly religious. In fact, Ben seemed outright against the whole idea. She assumed it was leftover residue from growing up in such a devout family.

"I am," Ben insisted. "Now listen, both of you. With Marius showing up, I realize that I can't keep this from you anymore. Marius is a tenacious asshole. If I tell you the truth, he can't use it against me. Please, I ask that you remember that you love me, and don't let your judgment of me be too harsh."

"Never." Noah sat next to him on the couch.

Jackie mirrored the sentiment and sat on the other side of him.

"I told you I ran with a different crowd when I was younger," Ben started. "My early twenties were not a great time, and it later led me to some dark places. I told you that much, but I didn't tell you what we were into." He stopped, waiting for Noah to say something. But his partner remained silent. Whatever Ben had to say, it weighed heavily upon him. So Noah would listen to every word.

"They were Satanists," Ben continued. "Not the Anton LaVey, Hollywood A-list types. And not the Midwestern metalhead ones either. These people believed in evil as everything—an archetype, a psychopomp, a spiritual essence, and a physical action.

They celebrated the Devil as something not removed from Heaven but not even associated with it. Hell, to them, was a place that did not exist as opposite from Heaven. The Ultimate Evil sat on a throne of agony and excrement, dispensing pain and loathing humans couldn't possibly comprehend.

"We did the usual things, like property defacement, scaring the pious, and celebrating anarchy like it was a practical philosophy. We did other things that I am not proud of." Ben winced at the cascade of memories, but he continued. "There were also rituals. Rituals that involved sacrifice."

Noah still said nothing. He waited patiently for Ben to continue.

"Rituals involved sacrifice; otherwise, they were just lip service. That's why the Catholics drink the blood of Christ and eat his flesh. They say that Christ died for their sins because it sounds better than what it really is—a sacrifice every Sunday for a thirsty God's favors.

"Then the dynamic changed. When I joined, there were a lot of 'meetings' they excluded me from. I didn't care because I was in it to appease my rage. At the time, I enjoyed screwing with people. When they explained to me the real story, I should have run right then. Instead, it made me want to stay and see what else would happen.

"They didn't actually believe in Satan. God and Satan to them were fairy tales and a convenient cover, something easier to explain. What they worshipped turned out to be so much worse." His mouth was dry, and his hands shook. He had never told another person about the group or what he had done with them. Too many times he wanted to tell Noah but chickened out. Ben took a sip of water, coughed when it tried to go down the wrong pipe and wiped his mouth as the fit subsided.

"What were they into, then, if not the Devil?" Jackie asked gently, not wanting him to stop. The importance of this confession filled the room; she did not want it to end until he purged it.

"They found an evil that made Satan look like the class clown. 'Verum Malum' they called it."

"True Evil," Noah intoned. Rusty as it was, he still remembered some Latin from college.

"Yes. And it is. The worst stories and ideas of Satan and Hell were just the beginning. The Verum Malum lives in a place that exists right outside our own plane of reality and sense of time. So when we die, if our souls go there, the torture lasts for eternity. The Verum Malum orchestrates it all, delighting in custom-made horror for each who enters its realm. We would often sit around and debate if we could raise it and call it to Earth. Marius didn't think so. All he wanted was power. The others wanted carnage. The evil of the world had an infinite battery in that place of the Verum Malum, and they wanted to unleash it. Rituals became more intense, releasing energies that scared me into believing they might be on to something.

"This cult, small but efficient, did not half-ass anything. The leader, an older man named Alexander, took everything seriously. He looked like a goofy shop teacher most days, but when he was 'about the great work,' he could be the scariest person on the planet. He initiated the ritual and wanted to commune with the evil himself. But we had to take baby steps. There were tales of groups, including the Nazis, that had raised the Malum. In every case, it ended badly for everyone involved. Instead he tried to summon a demon, bind it to us, and have it do our bidding.

"We pledged our souls to the Malum. Regardless of what we did in life, our souls are tied to its eternal misery upon death. We sealed the pact with blood and sex." Ben watched Noah for a reaction, but none came, so he continued. "We weren't a big group. Six of us in total. Jacob and Parker were two younger guys, cousins that enjoyed causing pain. Scarlet enjoyed seeing others bleed. Marius, you met. Alexander was in charge. Marius and Alexander were in it for a higher purpose that I almost understood. But they scared me.

"Why were you into it?" Noah asked. He didn't judge; he just wanted to understand.

"I was heavy into self-loathing at the time," Ben told him. "My parents were too busy hating what I was to care much for me, and I had nothing positive in my life. It seemed like fun. I had anger, and it was addictive to stoke the fire and extinguish it with all the wrong things."

"Just because you light a few candles and say some dark words doesn't mean you pledged your soul to anything," Jackie said.

"When we promised ourselves to the Malum," Ben said, struggling for a moment, "we…we did more than chant. We had to seal the deal with blood, spit, and cum. It was an orgy of pain and pleasure. We sliced our palms and spoke the pact aloud at the very end. I slid the knife along my palm, and as the blood welled up through the wound, it sizzled and spat like it was on a frying pan. I burned like fires were in my blood and tasted, for the tiniest sliver of a moment, what eternal torment waited for me. We were idiots, and we rode it like a high rather than a warning.

"Alexander wheeled the boy in, only a couple years younger than me. He was high as hell on some low-grade heroin. The sigils and glyphs were still fresh on the ground, and we were pumped up on our recent sacrifice of our souls. We laid him out and tied him down, naked except for a giant symbol on his chest. We began the chants and movements required. After that we raised the demon. Alexander let the cousins administer pain to our naked sacrifice until it was time for the knife. My job was to keep the chant going no matter what. I repeated the words as Alexander cut the boy open with precision, autopsy style. The others pulled out his guts and arranged them in the proper spots on the floor. I watched it all and continued chanting, louder and louder, hoping to drown out the boy's screams of pain. Scarlet and Marius drew symbols with the blood that flowed across the floor.

"Scarlet cut the boy's penis off and fed it into his now-silent mouth, laughing as she rubbed her crotch on his slack face. It was then that the candles stopped flickering and stood vertical and unmoving. The air became thick and claustrophobic. I continued my chant until I realized something was chanting along with me, a deep, scraping voice almost beyond my hearing. I looked to the others. None of them made a sound. We all watched the body and listened as the voice grew and grew…until it echoed off the walls, loud as my own.

"The body jerked once, then twice. Out of the cavity came a black shape, blacker than the night. It looked both solid and wispy at the same time. Red eyes burned as they looked at each of us in turn. We had raised a demon, Noah. This wasn't some middle school Ouija board bullshit. We brought a creature out of the Malum." He scanned Noah's face for a reaction.

Noah had the look of academic interest, but it didn't fool Ben. He knew well enough that wheels were turning in his partner's head, that there was nothing passive about his listening.

"What happened next?" Jackie asked. Ben trusted her to withhold her judgment until the end of his story.

"I felt sick and exhilarated at the same moment. The ultimate taboo had emerged. I was terrified and excited. In a voice that rode the wind like the scent of heavy garbage, the demon asked us what we wanted. That was the first time I stopped to consider what we had done. Before, it was the dark joy of being 'bad.' Then it was the heat of the moment. Even as they cut the boy up and spread him across the floor, I was so caught up in the chant, like some dark zen moment, I didn't acknowledge what was happening in front of me. It never occurred to me what we would do once we raised the demon, only that we tried to do it.

"Alexander and Marius had plans, though. They knew what they wanted. They bombarded the dark creature with questions. Jacob and Scarlet giggled at what they had wrought. It was as if I had emerged from a dream, reality crashing down. Fear crawled around inside me. Then the others started acting strange. Parker ate the boy's entrails off the dirty floor. Alexander stripped off his robe and sliced little cuts on his body as he engaged the creature. Jacob laughed louder and more maniacally until blood dribbled from his ears and nose. He coughed once and fell to the floor in a dead heap. Scarlet, her laughter ceasing, just stood there in awe. She looked rapturous and pounced on the open body on the floor. Marius was the only one that seemed unaffected; he continued asking the demon questions about what it could and couldn't do. He wanted control of it and what it had access to.

"My fear became too much, so I started backing away. I was sick to my soul. As I retreated, the demon turned to me. It said, 'You have all pledged your souls to something you know nothing about. I have never seen a bigger group of fools.'

"As it spoke, it began to fade. Marius and Alexander tried to strengthen the connection. With Jacob dead, Parker still rooting around in entrails, and Scarlet nearly orgasming from the demon's presence, their hold on it weakened. Plus, I don't think it could survive long here. It is made of different stuff than humans.

"After that, I ran out. I disappeared for a while, making sure no one was after me. I moved around for a couple years until I came here and met you." Ben sighed, exhausted from the story. He felt lighter light for it, telling someone his darkest secret, but some weight remained.

"That was a long time ago," Noah told him.

"Do you believe me?" Ben asked. It was important that Noah did, but he didn't hold high hopes.

Noah chose his words with care. The detail with which Ben had told his tale left him with imagery he would not soon forget. He decided to focus on being supportive first and process what he had just heard later.

"I believe you in all the parts I can. Like I said, it was a long time ago in a life that is no longer yours. Let's concentrate on now."

Ben squeezed Noah's hand, wanting more from him. But Noah didn't want to tell Ben how much the story scared him. Did he really raise a demon? Did he really see so much carnage? Watching Ben recount the memory, Noah saw that Ben believed every word he spoke. It unnerved him that he wasn't sure if he could believe what Ben had told him. A man he had always trusted.

Regardless of how unnerved he was, the fact that his husband lived such a dangerous life with such a deep darkness didn't scare him. This old life encroaching on their life now did scare him, however. Almost losing him to a disease was hard enough. He didn't want to lose him to some psychos from the past.

Jackie kept her thoughts to herself. The grisly details didn't bother her so much, and Ben was not one to lie. So she had no reason not to believe him. His account was as he experienced it, and what really happened wasn't important. She understood reality was reliant upon perception, and just because he believed, that didn't mean she had to. She was here when a friend needed to relieve a burden, and that was what mattered. She smiled and put her hand on Ben's.

"That was the person you were, and this is the person you are now. Whatever demons you may have raised, you live with an angel now."

IV

JASON, GUITARIST AND LEAD growler for the band Emaciated Angel, sprawled on his bed with his battered black guitar across his bare chest. He plucked at it with lazy fingers, the strings making muted, tinny sounds. His long brown hair fanned out under him. On the small television he watched an old Hammer film in which a very British Satan tempted blond nymphs to do his bidding.

Jason knew he should be practicing his shredding. His band had a gig coming up next weekend, and he had to make sure his hands were the fastest ones on stage. But he lay there hungry and stoned instead. He just wasn't feeling it tonight. Putting on a cheesy devil flick and smoking a bowl seemed like a better idea.

As a card-carrying Satanist, it's something he could easily justify. Living for the moment and doing what he damn well pleased was all part of being a follower of the Dark One. The music his band played was evil. He shunned religion, conventional society, and performed all the rituals out of the books he bought

43

from the bookstores. He could take a night off. But tonight, he needed to justify his laziness.

Something hung in the air like dark forces were lining up. He and his bandmates performed a ritual to raise the Devil a couple of nights ago. Nothing happened, even though that asshole Marius said they were on the right track. Jason didn't doubt that Marius laughed at them behind their backs.

"Elitist prick," Jason mumbled. "Marius thinks he's big shit, but he's some suburbanite who pretends he has tea and crumpets with demons all the time."

Regardless, Jason still felt something. He sat up and shredded through a quick pentatonic scale. He made a decision while searching the grungy covers of his bed for the phone. He dialed up his drummer to call a practice. If evil was in the air, they might use it to write some new songs. They needed some choice tracks if they planned to record a new album.

"Tim, it's Jason." He laid back down, switching to speakerphone and placing the device on his thin chest. "Let's have a practice. Something is up tonight, and we might be able to use it."

"Man, I am balls deep in someone right now," Tim said on the other end.

"Why the fuck did you answer the phone?" Jason laughed.

A woman said something on the other end, but her voice was too faint to make out the words. Before he hung up, his phone chirped. Lifting his head, he saw the name of an incoming call. "Shit, it's Alexander. Call me after you nut."

Jason picked up the phone and switched the call.

"Jason, how are you this evening?" Alexander always tried to sound so sophisticated on the phone, as if he were the Hammer-style Devil that smirked his way across Jason's flickering TV screen.

"What's up?" Jason sat up and leaned against the cool wall. Alexander only called when he needed something, and Jason already knew what it was.

"It seems my memory is faulty tonight. I'm trying to remember what it is you promised to do for me…"

"Alexander, listen, I can explain—"

"I know it had to be important and that you and your little group of musicians swore that you would get it done. On time, every time."

"We are a little late, but—"

"Oh, that's right, it's starting to come back to me. You are supposed to give me money." All pretenses of mock-politeness fell away as Alexander continued in calm, venomous tones. "And it seems we haven't seen a damned cent. You are late."

"Listen, I'm sorry, okay. But it's not like this shit is the hip thing right now. Only so many people are either brave enough or stupid enough to try your little evil spell kits. Sure, the drugs are easier, but since you left it to us to find our own supplier, we're in-between sources. Jake, the bassist, has a lead." Jason wiped nervous sweat from his brow.

"But I've received no money," Alexander's calm voice continued.

"I have your money. At least from what we've sold."

Jason waited for a reply. When he received none, he took the phone away from his ear. Alexander had hung up. "Shit."

He stood, leaning his guitar into its stand. He searched the floor for a black t-shirt to slip on. The phone lit up again.

"Tim, I hope you've nutted. I just got a call from Alexander," Jason said by way of a hello.

"Yeah, about that," Tim said, his voice higher than usual. "Do you have his money for him?"

"Only what we've made so far. Why? Did that asshole call you too?" Jason shoved the phone between his ear and shoulder as he opened the bottom drawer of his dresser. From underneath nudie magazines he pulled out a wooden cigar box with crude pentagrams carved into the top.

"Not exactly. That chick I was just in, well…eep…watch that thing," Tim said to someone on his end. "Well, it's Scarlet."

"Dude, that chick is seriously nuts. Don't stick your dick in crazy. How many times do I have to tell you?" Jason chuckled. He had contemplated doing the very same thing a couple times. But he figured that anyone part of Alexander's little coterie had to be insane.

"Man, she's still here. And she has a very sharp knife on my cock." Tim gasped. "Dude, promise that you'll get these fuckers their money tonight."

"I will shorten him inch by inch if you don't," Scarlet's faraway voice came through the phone. "And we both know this bald bastard has only two things, his drumming and this large pecker."

"Without those, I'm nothing," Tim squealed. "Tell her you're on your way."

"For Hell's sake," Jason muttered. "Yes, I am heading out the door now. Don't let her cut anything off. That monster between your legs is the only thing that keeps us in groupies." Swearing profusely, Jason hung up the phone. He opened the box to reveal a small stack of cash, some scraps of paper, a baggy of stale skunk weed, and some pills. He stared at the cash for a moment before slamming the lid and taking the entire box. Hotshot guitarist or not, he attended to business.

The scraps of paper were his accounting of all the shit they had shilled out for Alexander and his group of assholes. If they didn't like the way the band handled business, they could take the cash and the drugs back. All the spell kits and evil googaws they hadn't yet sold to bored suburbanite teenagers—he'd happily give them back, too.

Despite Alexander's right-hand man being an even bigger prick, Marius had been quite the fan of the band and brought them all into the fold. They became de facto members of the cult, although they were often reminded they were not part of the inner circle. Being amateur worshippers of Satan, the entire band nearly pissed themselves for the chance to be part of a real cult. Jason understood that these were some evil folks, and they meant business. When Marius approached them to help the cult make some money, it seemed like a good idea.

Doing shows around the city, they talked to a myriad of people. Each show had a merch table that sold the shitty handmade shirts and CDs they couldn't afford to make. Throwing in some of Alexander's crap along with it turned out to be the easiest way to move it. But they didn't have too many gigs this month, and to be honest, they were all losing interest in being the cult's little slaves.

He slipped on a scuffed pair of leather boots, sans socks, and clomped out of his room. In the sparse living room, Jake sprawled across the patched couch and watched some overly happy people selling useless plastic junk on TV. Lydia, the other guitarist, sat on the far end of the couch, her face illuminated from the white glow of her phone.

"C'mon, we have to go pay our *boss*," Jason growled as he stomped toward the door.

"It's late, man. We can do it tomorrow," Jake drawled, his eyes never leaving the set.

"Yeah. Screw him. He can wait another day," Lydia said, lips barely moving. Her drab, multi-hued hair bobbed, the only signs of life.

"Well, Tim banged Scarlet, and she's going to cut his dick off if Alexander doesn't get his money."

Jason wanted to strangle them both. If Lydia wasn't such a killer shredder and Jake the only bassist he found to keep up with Tim's nutso beats, he might have. They were the best bandmates in the world but refused to lift a finger to hold up their obligation to Alexander.

"I told him his dick would fall off if he had sex with her," Lydia tsked as she put her phone away and stood up.

Jake followed suit, making a show of grunting and stretching.

"Maybe Marius will show us the demon they claimed to have summoned," Lydia added as they left the house.

"All I'd like from him is to show us a little goddamned respect," Jason said as the door shut behind them.

An hour later, they were at the dark Victorian, and Jason wasn't sure if they were in good standing or not.

Marius and Alexander sat in their respective chairs while the band members stood there like kids called up on the carpet.

"So, despite your poor work ethic, we see it's time to give you a little more hands-on knowledge." Alexander's faux-regal air made Jason question why he ever took this guy seriously in the first place.

"You still have to make up for the amount you promised, on top of next month's," Marius made sure to remind them.

"I've got a guy lined up. It's good stuff, and it will sell. Don't worry," Jake blurted.

Alexander nodded at him.

"We'll call you when we plan our next ritual." Marius' impatience dripped from every word.

They were being dismissed.

"And you're summoning a demon? We get to see a demon?" Normally the no-nonsense one in the band, the cynical and take-no-shit one, Lydia's excitement made her look like an over-eager teenager.

Marius gave her a quick dismissive look. Jason wasn't sure if it was because of her excitement or her Asian features. He wondered if he might be getting overly sensitive, but he was learning that Marius didn't hide his prejudices well.

"We are summoning a demon, of course. And we'll be bringing a friend. Regarding that, we may ask a favor of you soon. Our friend will need an escort here. We'll call you," Alexander said with a wave of his hand.

Not one to hide his emotions, Jason did so now. His distaste for being treated like a servant grew. "Cool," he said. "You know where to find us." Then he looked toward the old staircase and called out, "Hey Tim! We're leaving! Let's go!"

"Hold on! I'm almost done!" Tim yelled down.

Jason rolled his eyes. He guessed Scarlet had put her knife away to finish what they had started earlier. Jason headed for the door. Tim knew his way home.

As they were leaving, Lydia stopped to ask Alexander a question. "Do you know a guy named Crazy Ned? He hangs out by the coffee shop downtown. Says he met the Devil once?"

"Many people claim to have met the Devil. Some even have," the older man said cryptically.

V

"GRUESOME," JACKIE SAID, WRINKLING her nose. She pushed the newspaper away. The only reason she had picked it up was because the table's previous occupant had left it behind. Noah opened it and looked at the story she had been reading.

"Who would murder anyone in a church?" Noah mused. "Man found ripped apart in the aisle of the church, and the priest found dead behind the altar. Hey, this church is right down the street."

They sat at a small bistro table in a busy upscale coffee shop called Bougie Brews. They'd had this weekly coffee date since Noah had moved in with Ben over three years ago. Noah and Jackie had been best friends since high school. They hid nothing from each other because Jackie would ferret it out of Noah anyway.

"My dad is investigating the case. Last night we had our obligatory once-a-month dinner. He mentioned the crime scene was the worst he had come across in years. One body torn into like an animal might have tried to get inside of it. This guy endured a lot of pain. The priest found the guy and most likely died of cardiac arrest at the sight. Like I said, gruesome," Jackie said, sipping her frothy vanilla latte.

"I didn't think he was supposed to talk about ongoing cases." Noah eyed the newspaper before him, trying not to envision the grisly details. If he kept the story in black and white print, his imagination wouldn't run amok with it. Plus, it brought up unwanted memories of Ben's recent confessions about his past.

"He's not, but he wanted me to leave early. He had a lady friend coming over. You'd think he'd learn by now. I was always interested in his work stories."

"You should have gone into police work," Noah said, pointing his coffee spoon at her.

"And not be able to express myself through an extravagant wardrobe? I think not." She twirled a bit of white lace with her finger. The pattern in the lace had grinning skulls on it. The dress had vibrant color splashes and prints of Halloween cats and broomsticks. Her style always tended toward the happy goth side of the spectrum, which always seemed to clash with Noah's usual accountant-esque look. "So, how's the art going? Working on any of your own stuff yet?"

Noah sloughed off his overcoat and adjusted the collar on his shirt. "Well, not really. I tried starting something the other night, but I'm too distracted. Not to mention I've been busy with commissions."

"Damn shame. You really need to do more of your own stuff. I'm serious, Noah. When left to your own devices, you come up with wild shit. Not to take away from all the covers you've done. But you know what I mean."

He did. But his own creative block ran deeper than the day-to-day work.

"Ben and I had a scare the other day. That was the real reason for the little party," he blurted out.

"You knocked him up?" Jackie's sarcasm was never quicker than when she worried.

"Someone crank called and pretended to be Ben's doctor—"

"Uncle Teddy?"

"Yes. The caller told me that Ben's cancer is back. When we got a hold of the real Uncle Teddy, he told us that everything is still clean."

"What sort of confuckled thundercunt would do such a thing!? I mean, you'd have to be a cock to the millionth magnitude to think that would be funny."

Jackie's anger roiled, and her voice started climbing higher. "If I find the asshole who made that call, it will be the end of him."

Noah sipped at his black coffee.

They sat for a quiet moment with their beverages while Jackie studied her best friend.

"What else is wrong? You can't hide your troubled little mind from me." She set her cup down and gave him the 'heavy stare.'

Noah couldn't resist it.

"I suspect Ben knows who made that phone call, and it might have been the guy he almost tore to pieces on our doorstep. He's keeping tight-lipped, though. When I ask him about it, he changes the subject. Why does he want to shut me out?"

"We almost lost him. It took a toll on all of us, Ben the most. Maybe he wants to deal with it his own way and save us the grief," Jackie suggested, taking the most optimistic route per usual.

"I hope so. I also wanted to ask you about what he told us regarding his past. I'm not so sure about it. Not that I don't believe him, but it's just so hard to accept. Ben is a good-natured person. Sure, he can have a temper and a dark streak, but he's always been a gentle person to me."

"You're the reason he's so gentle." Jackie put her hand on his. Her touch reassured him, but she could see that he still needed an actual opinion from her. "Listen, I'm not sure about it either. While it is extremely uncharacteristic of him, I can see it. He's an expansive person, someone who doesn't shy away from experiences. We all make weird decisions when we're young."

"But what he described…" Noah had been trying to get rid of the images Ben's memories had given him. They refused to go, and they disturbed him. As an artist of the dark and macabre, these sorts of images weren't unusual. That they came from his husband as a genuine experience turned out to be more troublesome than he expected. When Ben recounted the tale, he listened as a caring husband. Reflecting on it later left him more and more disturbed. They were so violent and visceral.

"We trust Ben. If he said it's true, then it is," she said distractedly watching something over his shoulder. "We also know he is a good person. He got into a bad situation, is all.

"You're right, and I do trust him completely, but demons and eviscerations? I dunno. Maybe he got high and had a bad trip. Or maybe it was true, and there is shit out there that is too horrifying to contemplate." He shook his head when he noticed her attention diverted.

"Crazy Ned is on the corner." Jackie nodded at the window behind him.

Noah peered out and recognized the man in the jean jacket and army-green hood. "Yep, appears so."

"I'll get him a coffee. Meet you out there."

Jackie stood and got back in line.

Noah got up, too, knowing that Jackie had changed the subject on purpose. He had the tendency to dwell, and sometimes his mind needed its channels changed.

Outside in the cool sunny morning, he approached the grizzled old man. He had known Crazy Ned for years, going back to when he used to work with Noah's father in the same shipping warehouse. That was before Ned lived on the streets and before Noah had come out to his family.

"…well, I was a hardworking man, you see." Crazy Ned's whispery gruff voice lilted on the city's breeze as he talked to two middle-aged tourists. "I thought to myself, there has to be more than this. More than working for a living, slaving for the man, and being unable to fulfill one's own destiny. So, I quit. Walked out and never looked back."

Noah had heard this story a million times, and the bent old man told it with the same pride every time. The two tourists, looking decidedly west coast, regarded him with admiration and pity. They thought the same thing all the others did—so brave to balk the system, but not strong enough to remain another cog in society's wheel.

"And what happened to your voice…if you don't mind me asking? Was it a work accident, or was it caused by living on the streets?" the woman asked, holding her purse close to her chest.

Crazy Ned scratched through the gray beard on his chin with a dirty finger. "My voice is like this because of my trip to Hell," he stated matter-of-factly. "Let me tell you about Hell. It ain't all fire and brimstone. I mean, it is, but there is so much more to it. You see all the things that pull at your soul, like all your sins and all your wrongs. But that's just the beginning. As you go deeper, you see rooms padded with all the gore that makes a human… Hey, where you goin'? You asked a damned question, and I'm giving you a damned answer," he hollered at the couple as they skittered away.

"No one wants to hear about the hereafter on a Monday, Ned," Noah said as he watched the couple disappear in the crowd.

"For the best. Our minds aren't attuned to it. They can't process what I have to tell them anyway." He saw Jackie approach with a steaming white cup. "You are gorgeous!"

"Thank you," Jackie said.

"I meant the coffee," Ned growled, shaking as he squeaked out his strange laugh. "Sugar?"

"All they had," she told him.

Ned nodded thanks and sipped at the steaming brew.

"We've been chasing off tourists again," Noah told her.

"Oh, so a typical Monday. Good." Jackie giggled. "How have you been? Haven't seen you in a couple weeks. I was getting worried."

"With that last cold snap, I had to find something indoors. Guy like me, with my lifestyle, pneumonia is a death sentence. Gotta put that off as long as I can."

"Don't want to go back to Hell," Noah said. He didn't tease or joke because of how serious Crazy Ned was about his supposed trip to the fiery afterworld. He and Jackie figured the guy had schizophrenia, and it was best to go with the flow. Crazy Ned had a reputation on the streets as someone not to mess with when his anger was up.

"I'm going back, don't kid yerself. You go once, you wind up there in the end, no matter what. Keep that in mind. Any dealings you have with that place and any of its residents will seal yer fate." The old man sipped his coffee between sentences. "This ain't some crazy homeless guy talk, either. I know this for a fact. My fate is sealed."

"We'll keep an eye out for demons, just to make sure," Jackie said with her accustomed cheer.

"It won't be easy. They sneak up, and ya won't know till it's too late," he answered Jackie but looked at Noah. "Thanks for the coffee."

And with that, he shambled down the street.

Jackie and Noah looked at each other and shrugged. Noting the time, the two said their goodbyes, Jackie promising to drop in the next day. Noah knew she did it because she needed to make sure they were okay. He felt blessed to have such a friend.

As Jackie and Noah walked in opposite directions, neither noticed the short, pale-haired young man leaning against a nearby light pole.

His eyes followed their every move as the distance between them grew. But when Jackie disappeared around the corner of the far building, he pushed himself off the pole and followed her to the closest bus stop. She was his sole focus now.

The pale-haired man came up and stood near her. He mumbled something, but she couldn't quite catch it. She had lived in big cities her entire life, so paying attention while acting like she wasn't became second nature. Experience told her mumblers were often not to be trusted.

"See, Jacob, I told you. Here we are. I told Alexander I could do it. I do it all the time. We're following the girl this time," he whispered just below her hearing.

Jackie turned and gave him the I-acknowledge-you-are-here smile. He looked up at her and returned the expression. It was a thin but inviting smile. Slick and infectious. Nice as it was, Jackie didn't trust it.

"Is this the uptown bus? Umm, 302, right?" he asked, all mumbling now forgotten.

Jackie pointed at the nearby sign. "Sure is. You're in the right spot."

"Good. I don't usually take the bus, so I get confused. My name is Parker, by the way. Do you take this bus a lot?"

"I take all the buses, all the time. But really, it's easier than driving my car all over town." Something about this guy made her uneasy. "Oh, speak of the devil," she said as the bus pulled up and came sighing to a stop.

As the doors opened, Parker waited for her to step on first.

"Please, go ahead. I need to dig my bus pass out." She turned and stuck her hands in her pockets, searching with vigor.

Parker stood there for a second before getting on the bus.

"Hey lady, you coming?" the bus driver barked a few seconds later.

Jackie waved her on. "Sorry, can't find it. I'll get the next one."

The driver shrugged and closed the doors, pulling off into traffic.

Jackie, hands still in her pockets, watched Parker stare at her from the window, his face an impassive mask. *What a weird guy,* she thought as she settled in to wait for the next one, bus pass in hand. The strangest part, she decided, it almost felt like a third person was standing with them.

VI

MARIUS AND ALEXANDER STOOD at opposite ends of the dark room. A thick fog of tension choked the air. Parker and Scarlet sat in the corner snickering at some private joke. While the men had become used to it, the members of Emaciated Angel were not, and it continued to heighten their already rising anxiety.

They all stood in the former dining room of the house. The windows, secured with paper and tape, let in no light. The wallpaper, most likely original to the house, bubbled and tore here and there. Dented molding and wainscoting were marked by years of abuse and neglect. A grimy atmosphere permeated the room. Jason hated it in here because of that fact. It always left him stifled and suffocated.

They did low-level rituals and ceremonies in this room. A pentagram surrounded by symbols was painted on the scarred wooden floor. Collecting dust on the wall there hung several effigies and symbols. Tonight, they used this room to prep for a much bigger ritual.

"We have a Great Work to do tonight," Alexander said as his pants hit the floor.

Everyone was to change from street clothes to the provided black robes. Jason looked away from Alexander. Not that he hadn't seen a naked fat man before, but everything about Alexander revolted him at that moment. Plus, the way he leered at Lydia's slim naked frame made him wonder if he did it just to see the girl unclothed. Scarlet and Parker were already naked when the rest entered the room, their robes flung across their shoulders.

Once they were all dressed, Alexander continued. "Tonight, we will commune with an old friend. Years ago, we spoke to this entity, and it is time to call on it again."

Scarlet and Parker exchanged nervous looks.

"Are we raising the demon?" Jake asked. He leaned against the wall, trying to play it cool, but everyone saw his nervousness.

"No." Marius stepped forward, causing Alexander to frown at the interruption. "We will not be raising it tonight. We are missing one key element for that. Tonight, we only open a line of communication. We will hail it and ask questions. The answers will prepare us for an even bigger endeavor."

"Our last encounter proved that we needed more knowledge if we were to raise and contain such a being." Alexander took a step beyond Marius. "Tonight is also a test for you. Your dedication is acknowledged, if not a little lazy on your end of the bargain."

Jason bristled at the latter but said nothing.

"If you have the fortitude for such a ritual," Alexander continued, "you will be worthy of bigger undertakings."

"We won't let you down," Jason said, then looked at his band.

Tim, cowl covering his bald head, gave Jason an idea for their next album cover. Jake still looked nervous, but he had always been the nervous type. He would fidget and fret before a show, but as soon as he hit the stage, he owned it. Lydia had her usual cool countenance on. She wore it as comfortably as she wore the robe. It didn't fool Jason, though; she was like a kid in a candy store right now. He respected Lydia as a musician, and because she knew as much about demonic undertakings as he did, possibly more.

"I know you won't," Marius said with more than a little malice. "Come."

He led them out of the room to sagging wooden stairs leading to the basement. One by one, they descended. The basement's humid air clung to them. Across from the stairs sat a rusty water heater and furnace, both well past their prime. Dust and mildew covered the concrete floor. At the far end sat a wooden door, crooked with age. It screeched as Marius forced it open. Inside they saw burning candles.

As they stepped in, the air cooled and thinned. The atmosphere changed, and the hair on everyone's neck rose.

"We've already done some preparation," Alexander explained as his group took their places.

As everyone's eyes adjusted to the candlelit gloom, Lydia gasped, and Jake swore. In the hexagon lay a prone naked body, restrained by chains, painted with symbols. A black sack covered his head.

"Who is this guy?" Jason asked, surprised by what he saw. A hooded, tied-up person in the middle of symbols on the floor usually meant someone wasn't leaving on their own by the end of the night.

"Our cipher, or sacrifice, however you want to think of it," Marius explained as he ushered the others to their spots. "We normally only need six for the ritual, so one of the extras stands here, and the other here. You will strengthen our barriers. That way, if anything else tries to break through, they will have to go through you first."

Jake and Tim stood off point with Parker in-between them. Parker gave them a wicked smile before mumbling something into his shoulder. A chill ran up Jake's spine.

Scarlet's hungry eyes locked onto the young man in the hexagram. Jason looked at her, and his skin crawled. None of this sat well with him. It lacked the usual satanic trappings: goats' heads, pentagrams, altars covered in blood-red wax. On paper, a human sacrifice looked good, but right in front of his eyes, he wasn't so sure now.

"Is he drugged?" Jason asked, dancing around his real concerns.

"Yes," Marius said, his smile amping up Jason's discomfort. "They are much more receptive when they are in a drugged state. Plus, they make a lot less noise."

"I still wanted to pick up that Latino kid," Scarlet pouted, making even that expression appear sinister.

"Scarlet, I am not having some half-assed ritual. If we are going to have a sacrifice, I want it to be of some value," Marius barked at her.

Jason and Lydia shared a look. Marius's free-range racism, always noticeable under the surface, now became all too clear. Lydia shifted, her eyes glancing at the door. If Marius or any of the others started that purity shit with her, Jason decided that he would have to sort them out. Great evil power or not, you don't fuck with a person's bandmates.

"You're not going to kill him, right?" Jason finally asked.

"You can't have a sacrifice without blood. Nor can you talk to demons without releasing the appropriate energies," Alexander snipped. "Now, let's get on with it."

With that, the main group, already practiced in their roles, bowed their heads and started chanting in low voices.

"Umm…what do you need us to do?" Tim tapped his hands against his legs, already tired of standing there and doing nothing.

70

"In your mind, focus on the demon. Keep concentrating on summoning it through our cipher here." Marius pointed at the young man. "And imagine it rising to meet us. You can chant the following if you like: 'Daemon intus, exsurge, et loquere nobis. Loquere de malis regni tui vilis et nostris quaestionibus responde. Non potes nocere nobis hic.' Latin is so archaic, yet it still seems to get the best results."

"Okaaay…" Tim blinked.

"Or use the English translation. Whatever works for you," Marius added before bowing his head to chant.

The members of Emaciated Angel exchanged looks and tried to emulate the others as much as possible.

Minutes passed. The air swirled around them in ribbons of cool fetid movement. Jason tried to locate the source of the breeze but found none. The candles flickered but did not go out. Other than the drone of the low chants, the only other sound was the occasional whimpering of the young man in the middle. He made feeble attempts to move his arms and legs. Though Jason wanted to pretend the guy wasn't there, he couldn't.

The pressure in the room changed. The air thickened. Louder, in a mixture of various languages,

Alexander started chanting something over the others. He spread his arms wide. The sacrifice whimpered louder and squirmed. Parker and Scarlet's hungry eyes focused on the cipher. They wanted to inflict pain and torture. To them, it was like sex, Jason realized. Alexander's face took on a rapturous countenance as he continued to get louder and louder. In response, the air grew thicker and thicker.

Jason feared he wouldn't be able to breathe and wanted to run. He turned to Lydia, who seemed caught up in it all. She wanted to see the demon. Tim and Jake were too busy trying to figure out the chant. Their faces scrunched in concentration as if trying to learn a complicated riff. Marius' eyes were on Alexander, and it alarmed Jason, though he couldn't figure out why.

We are in over our heads, he thought as he eyeballed the door behind Alexander.

A low droning sound surrounded them. All attention snapped to the bound man. His back arched high, his fingers locked into claws, and his erection poked upwards. The sound came from his open mouth, a deep moan that no normal larynx could naturally produce.

"Now is the time. Make the cuts. Ready yourselves. We have only as long as the sacrifice clings to life to hold the demon," Alexander instructed, his high ecstatic voice betraying his excitement.

Scarlet, knife in hand, approached the center. Jason had never seen such a predatory look on a person before. Tim saw the knife and shivered, his hands covering his crotch.

"Steady your hand," Marius warned her.

She didn't acknowledge him but obeyed all the same. Tracing the painted symbols on his body, Scarlet cut each one deep. Blood seeped out, yet the man did not trash or move. He maintained the arched position, the droning still coming from his mouth. When she finished, she stepped back, her knife dripping crimson.

"Will the demon come? There has been no death offering," Parker said, disappointed no one had died yet.

"Oh yes, we can't forget that," Alexander chuckled.

Jason and the rest of the band stood stock still. Each one thinking the same thing. Tim had already taken a half-step toward Lydia. Jason planned to go through Alexander if he had to. And Jake was sizing up Marius. Lydia, fist balled up, was ready to battle her way out. They weren't going down without a fight. That wouldn't be very metal of them.

"Yes, we can't forget that, can we?"

Marius' knife flashed in the candlelight before passing across Alexander's thick neck.

Time froze, hushed surprise taking temporary ownership of the room.

Confusion and shock passed over the sliced man's face before a line of red spilled down his chest. He grabbed his neck with one hand and Marius with the other.

Marius shrugged him off, letting him fall to the ground. Blood flowed black across the concrete floor.

"What the fuck!?" Scarlet and Parker shouted in unison.

"We needed a sacrifice, and we got one." Marius wiped the knife on his robes. "I dedicate this sacrifice to Oronus, the demon of the Malum. You have been to Earth before, Oronus, and we wish you to speak through our cipher. The blood given is yours!"

"But Alexander…" Parker said, unsure what to do next.

"He was a weak link. Ambition stopped short with him. Causing discord, tapping into the most minimal amounts of dark energies, and dallying with demons— that's as far as he wanted to go. We have something much more powerful than Hell at our disposal. Why should we just get a taste of it when we can have the whole thing. Are you with me?"

Marius waited for their answers. As he did, the blood from their now-deceased leader reached the cipher. The droning changed. It sounded closer now, the pitch climbing higher.

"Choose now. We have a guest arriving." Marius' smile took over his whole face. He smelled triumph before it presented itself.

Scarlet nodded, the hunger returning to her eyes as she watched the cipher. Parker assented as well, giving Alexander's body one more look before observing the cipher too. The others watched the drama unfold with wide eyes.

Jason mouthed two words to his bandmates: *Play along*. They nodded and turned their attention to the ritual.

"Oronus!" Marius called out.

"That is not my name," a deep wavering voice oozed from the cipher's open mouth. "You called me that name last we met. It is not my name."

"We gave you a name to gain control," Marius said, his eyes wide with victory.

"You are amusing, human," the voice said. "You are also stupid. There is so much you don't understand."

"Time for you to educate us then."

As Marius spoke those words, Jason knew they were all doomed.

VII

"WHAT IS THE WORST these guys can do?" Noah asked Ben.

The clink of silverware and glass surrounded them. It had been months since the two of them had gone out to dinner. Ben had suggested it, and Noah hadn't bothered to hide his relief. Restlessness had taken hold of Ben in a big way since the stranger showed up on their doorstep. He wandered the house irritable and pensive. Noah tried to get him to talk about it, but Ben either refused or brushed it off every time. Now, confined to a booth at their favorite steak house, Noah asked his questions.

"More than you know," Ben said before popping a forkful of broccoli in his mouth.

Noah stared at him expectantly as he chewed. Then Ben chewed slower and slower, exaggerating it even more until Noah realized he was being amusingly irritating.

"I have all night, sweetheart. You just enjoy that food." Noah winked at him and smiled.

Ben swallowed and took a drink of water. He wanted a merlot but didn't partake for Noah's benefit. "I'm not getting out of this, am I?"

Noah shook his head.

"Okay. You're right. I've mixed you up in this. I lied to myself, thinking I was free, but I'm not."

"At least tell me what to expect. If they are as dangerous as you keep implying, we can always call the police."

"It won't help, and let's be honest, how much help will they give us?" Ben raised a dark eyebrow.

Noah had no argument for that. They were both dark-skinned and in a same-sex marriage. Their dealings with the local police had not gone well in the past. Early in their relationship, someone broke into Ben's car. They called the police, and when the officers showed up, they had more questions about his Lebanese heritage than the break-in. Noah, who had stayed quiet up to that point, objected to the line of questioning and had the suspicion turned to him. Suddenly his Cuban relatives were the most likely suspects.

What bugged Noah the most about the whole encounter wasn't the line of questioning or even that nothing was done about the crime. It was the fact that the racist cop's partner, who attempted to do his job and acted friendly to them, did nothing to quell the belligerency.

"Fine, no police. But what are these people capable of? How can we protect ourselves if they harass you again?"

"We kill them on site."

The statement shocked Noah. Not that Ben had said it, but how serious it came out.

"Listen, I know how driven they are. Killing someone does not weigh on their conscience at all. In fact, most of them get off on it. Marius showing up at the house is a message. They want me back in the fold. I can guess what they are planning, too. Otherwise, they wouldn't need me."

"Calling on the demon?" Noah's tone was skeptical in the politest of ways. He put a forkful of baked potato in his mouth.

"I know you don't believe me, but it's the truth. I know what I saw. Either they are trying to recreate the same situation or take it to the next level. To do that, they need all the same elements in place," Ben said, then waited for a response. The look on his husband's face told him that Noah was searching for the right words. "These people pose a threat."

"These Satanists exist, and you ran with them back in the day, I'll concede that. Demons and this 'Verum Malum,' a Hell worse than Hell, I'm not so sure about that. For being raised Catholic, I never took to it. So, in my mind, this is another one of my commissions. That band, Emaciated Angel, it's a scene for their next album cover. But on the other hand, you wouldn't lie to me. I trust you more than anyone else. If you say they are a threat, and if you say you met a demon, I'll go with it. The big question is: What do we do about it?"

Ben sighed and put down the fork. "My gut reaction is to run, but that's not a long-term solution. I have a job, we have friends, and they would find me anyway. I can try to reason with them, tell them I wouldn't do them any good. They want a ritual, and they want me to be the sacrifice, most likely. Anything they tried to make me do I would intentionally ruin. But it may get ugly, and I don't want you to get caught in the crossfire."

"Hon," Noah looked his husband in the eye, "they have to get through me first."

Ben smiled. He could not have loved Noah more than he did at that moment. He could not have been more depressed either. Marius would flay him alive, chain him down, and surround him with magical symbols. Chances were, they would give Noah to Scarlet for the fun of it. Ben saw no scenario that ended well, not without confronting them head-on, not without blood being spilled.

After dinner, they went for a short walk and then returned home. Ben tried not to brood, and Noah tried not to notice for his sake. When they both crawled into bed, each did so with a sense of foreboding. Ben wanted to put off the inevitable confrontation, wanted to avoid facing his past. Noah wanted to protect Ben, but he wasn't sure how.

JASON, TIM, LYDIA, AND Jake all huddled around a chipped table in an all-night diner, steaming mugs of coffee in their hands. Each stared off at some point a million miles away. No one spoke for a few minutes. What was the point? They all shared the same thoughts. What they had just experienced defied all expectations and changed their view of reality.

"What. The. Fuck?" Lydia finally whispered.

"Yeah," the others agreed.

"I wanted to see a demon. I really did. But what we saw is not what I had in mind." She sipped her coffee.

"Why in the hell did we agree to that? Why did we ever hook up with these psychopaths?"

No one answered Jake's rhetorical question. They already had the answer, but it was all too fresh to reconcile the naivety that kept them with Marius' group up to now.

"What. The. Fuck?" Lydia asked again.

The waitress came by to refill coffee, and Tim ordered a slice of pie out of habit. The rest sat trying to forget their evening but could not stop the flow of images.

When the demon's voice emerged from the boy's mouth, time had stopped. A stifling sense of forever pervaded them. Fear of never leaving this moment in time struck them all. An idea of invisibility also came to them. As if the Demon was aware that they were there, but not. The sensation, disturbing as it was, also afforded them the only mote of comfort they would have during the entire affair.

"Oronus, we have called you here to answer our questions. We have called you here to help us achieve something no other human dared do," Marius began, his glee breaking through his usual commanding demeanor. "You will do our bidding while still in your domain."

"I will answer your questions, but you will not like my answers. As for your supposed 'achievements,' you will not get what you want. No humans do," the demon said. The cipher's back still arched, his muscles still locked. "In the end, you will do me a favor. Like for like. Do you agree?"

"I agree," Marius said, clapping his hands together. A second later, the room shook with a thunderous clap that seemed to come from the bowels of Hell itself. "We have come to an agreement, and both parties shall honor said agreement. Now tell us, demon, how does one go to the Malum?"

"Those who wish to go will. Those who feel it's what they deserve will go. You humans are such masochists. One little 'bad' thing and the impulse buries itself in your shallow little psyches. To come against your will means you have generated insurmountable amounts of horrible energies in the world. And the Verum Malum is always happy to take you in."

"I...I'm confused," Lydia said.

Marius looked up at her, burning with hatred because of her interruption. Both Scarlet and Parker were poised, ready to pounce on her if instructed.

"Aren't we talking to a demon from Hell? What about Satan?" she asked.

"Same concepts, but different," Marius said, trying to regain what momentum he had lost.

"The Verum Malum is not Hell. Nor is it Satan," the demon said. It cared little for who asked the questions. A hint of delight in its voice increased Marius' ire. "The Verum Malum has nothing to do with earthly religious notions. It is a plane of pure pain and suffering. The Malum itself rules, concocting tortures and eternities of horror for the realm's inhabitance. The Malum is not Satan, for it never came from 'Heaven.' Nor does it acknowledge any 'God.' It exists, and you humans show up...if you're so inclined. There is no concept of time in the Malum, so there will never be an end."

"What if we don't want to go," Jake asked, surprised at his own question.

"Like I said, sometimes it gets implanted into your own psyche, whether you realize it or not."

"And sometimes you are marked by association," Marius said, making a point of meeting everyone's eyes.

The demon had no comment on this.

"Has anyone visited the Malum and come back?" Parker asked. An edge of desperation lined the question.

"A few have touched the boundaries. They were given a glimpse of it, and one or two didn't go *completely* mad, though they did not come back completely sane. One does not stare into the abyss and remain the same." Again, the demon's words showed some amusement on its part.

"How does one get 'touched' by the Malum here on Earth?" Marius got to the point. His time was being wasted by useless questions.

"Touched? You want power. Humans have this idea that the Malum can grant them evil powers to achieve dominion over others."

"Can it be done?"

The demon said nothing.

Marius asked again, this time yelling his question: "Can it be done?"

"The possibility is there," the demon said. "The Malum can 'touch' you, and you can consequently receive abilities otherwise unknown. But I assure you, the trip here and back to attempt such a thing would destroy you before you could use said abilities."

"You underestimate me, demon. Now tell me how? What must I do?"

"I cannot. Your time is almost up, as your cipher is almost dead. Once this body releases its soul, the connection will end."

"Wait, wait"—Marius didn't hide his desperation— "tell me what I need to know."

"There is no time!" The room shook from the thunderous words. "There is only time to tell you my side of the bargain. I answered your questions, now you must do this one thing for me. Raise me again, like you did before. But when you do, you must hold me in your realm."

"You can't survive here. That's why you were pulled back into the Malum the last time."

"There is a way to hold me here, to keep me from going back. I will not survive, but that is the goal. I wish to die on Earth, where I was born, not spend eternity with the Verum Malum, even though it is where I belong. To do this, you will need to—"

"I know what needs done." Marius' interruption caught the demon off guard. "I am aware of the rituals, and it may surprise you to know I have the knowledge and skills to grant your request. But I can't do it at this moment."

"YOU PROMISED!" Again, the room shook. Dust flittered from the ceiling and walls.

"I can't do it at this moment. I must have all the right elements in place and all the right people. I will hold up my bargain, Oronus. Have some patience." Marius nodded at Scarlet, who walked up to the cipher and plunged her knife into his heart.

The demon's yell cut off, and the cipher's body fell in a heap, his muscles finally able to relax in death.

"Hated to cut that call short, but no sense belaboring the point," Marius said, looking pointedly at Parker and Scarlet. "The full moon is coming soon, so we'll do the next ritual at that time. Ben will be our sacrifice.

It's fitting that he should help bring our demon back once and for all."

The trio exited the room and ascended the wooden stairs, leaving the bodies of the young man and Alexander there to lie. Jason and the others didn't move; they just stared.

"What was that?" Jason asked.

"You saw what you saw," Parker shot back at him. "Don't be stupid."

"But the bodies…I mean…and…" Jason floundered for words, his mind still trying to grapple with his sense of reality.

"Don't worry about that," Marius said from the stairs. He nodded at Parker and Scarlet. "These two can handle it just fine. But I will require your services. Nothing so visceral as this. I'll need you to pick up someone and escort them here. I'll call you with the details."

In the diner, the four musicians sat there processing their evening. Coffee cups were now empty, and the pie eaten, but Tim tasted little of it.

"I'm not doing any more errands for them," Jake said, pushing himself away from the table. "I'm done with that horror show. We should all walk away."

The others nodded, except for Jason.

"Walking away may not be an option right now," he said. "You saw the same shit I did. These aren't Hollywood devil worshippers. They have tapped into something worse. I'm not sure 'no' is an option available to us anymore."

"What do we do?" Jake stood up.

"Let me handle it." Jason rubbed his face, exhaustion taking its toll. "I might run some interference. Do little things, like getting this guy for them. We can slip under Marius' radar while he plays with his demon." He stood up. "I got us into this. It was my big idea to join up with them. I'll get us out."

Tim stood too, and the others started walking toward the exit. Lydia remained seated, staring at the bottom of her empty mug. "What if he succeeds? What if he gets the powers he's looking for?"

"You heard that thing. No one survives. Humans can't handle it," Jason assured her, hoping what the demon said was true.

She stood up. "You better be right, or we're all in a world of shit."

VIII

"ARE YOU SURE YOU'RE okay? You seem distant today." Noah looked at Ben from across the table.

They sat at Bougie Brews, in their usual side booth. Jackie had dragged them both out of the house despite the fact that neither had the patience to deal with the public. She sensed the worry and tension and decided getting them out might help. As soon as she excused herself to use the restroom, Noah pounced on Ben's mood.

"I'm fine," Ben lied.

But Noah saw right through it. In the last few days, Ben had said little, ate less, and slept barely at all. They had been through this once before—right after Ben received his initial cancer diagnosis. Only Uncle Teddy's adamant insistence on Ben's clean bill of health convinced him that he still lived in remission.

"With all due respect, my love, I am going to call bullshit." Staring until Ben caught his eye, Noah held his husband's gaze until he surrendered.

"Fine. I'm just waiting for the other shoe to drop, I guess. I get this sense that someone will show up out of nowhere, and things will get ugly. It's getting to a point that I wish they would so I can get it over with," Ben admitted.

It had gotten so bad that he lay in bed and weighed the idea of going to find Alexander and Marius before they came for him.

"Don't wish that." Noah frowned and put his hand on Ben's.

"You know what I mean. I hate the anticipation."

"What are we anticipating?" Jackie said, taking her seat next to Ben.

"We were talking about what I'm going to do to him once I get him home and in bed," Noah deflected.

Jackie put her head in her hands and rested her elbows on the table. She batted her eyelashes at Noah. "Please be descriptive. You forget that I wrote gay erotic fan fiction in college."

They laughed and took sips of their coffee, but it didn't dispel the gloom that surrounded them.

"So, what are we going to do about it?" Jackie said, jolting the other two out of their reveries.

"Do about what?" Ben asked, pushing his coffee away. Any more and he'd be jittery all day.

"You two are moping around like the weight of the world is on your shoulders. I suspect it has something to do with these demonic bastards you used to run with. So, I ask again: What are we going to do about it?"

"I'm not sure we can do anything. I didn't even know they were in town," Ben said after a moment's thought. "They want me back, and I refuse to go. To force a confrontation would only play into their hands."

They had him backed into a corner, and he hated it. He couldn't run, he couldn't confront them, and he couldn't ignore them forever. The potential of putting Noah in danger worried him the most.

While Noah finished his coffee, Jackie grilled Ben with questions. Being raised by a homicide detective had made its mark on her. Ben revealed more of his activities that he had not already confessed to her. He admitted to aiding in robberies, assaults, and vandalism. He once watched Scarlet kill someone because they dared cross Alexander. His inaction to stop her made him feel as guilty as if he had done it himself. Even if he hadn't pledged his soul to the Malum, he felt he would still be damned.

Coffees finished, the three stepped outside into the gray afternoon. Once again, Crazy Ned stood at his corner talking with everyone who walked by.

"Isn't that one of the guys from the band?" Ben pointed at the long-haired man speaking with Ned.

Noah didn't ask which band. Since doing artwork for Emaciated Angel, they were forever known as 'the band.'

"It is." Noah started walking over. "I should see if they need anything new made up. Never hurts to drum up some business."

Ben followed while Jackie walked back to get Ned his obligatory overly sweet coffee.

As they approached, the two heard Ned's raspy voice detailing his favorite subject.

"I'm sure you talk a lot about Hell in that music you make, but you have no idea about the real thing."

"I wanted to talk to you about that. I had this experience, and you said you did too." Jason stopped when he saw Ben and Noah approach. He gave Ben a double take, the color draining from his face. That very morning, Marius called him and instructed him to bring Ben to the house. Jason had waffled, trying to get out of it, but Marius gave him no outs. Arming him with a home address, a picture, and places Ben liked to frequent, Marius had given him until midnight to have him on the doorstep.

Jason stalled as long as he could by first stopping at the most frequented places. He didn't want to do this and wasn't sure what he would do if Ben refused. He drove by the coffee shop first and spied Crazy Ned. Talking with the homeless man would be a welcome distraction.

"Funny meeting you here," Noah said, putting his hand out to shake.

Jason didn't take it, his eyes still locked on Ben.

"You okay?" Noah put his hand down after a moment.

"Run!" Jason blurted. The word surprised even him. "He sent me to bring you back, but I can't. The dude is playing with shit he can't hope to control, and he wants you back."

"Alexander," Ben said, knowing without asking.

"Marius killed him. He's out of his damned mind."

Ben's jaw clenched. Alexander always kept Marius in check. The need to run outweighed all other options. If he made it too much trouble for Marius to come after him, maybe he would lose interest.

He turned to Noah. "We need to go."

"Listen," Jason stopped him. "I can try to stall him a little. But you gotta get as far away as—"

"As what?" Scarlet's unexpected voice stopped everyone in their tracks. "Ben, long time since I laid eyes on you."

Everyone turned as she approached them from the street.

Parker walked beside her, a smug grin on his face. "You won't get far."

"You fucked up, you dumb metalhead," Parker said to Jason. "You should have done your job."

"I'm not coming with you," Ben said. He couldn't imagine how much more dangerous Scarlet had become over the years.

"You are." She flicked a gaze at Noah. "Since he's here, why don't you both come? We have an evening planned with you as our guest of honor, Ben. You wouldn't want to miss that, would you?"

Noah stepped in front of Ben. "You aren't taking him anywhere, not without going through me."

"Okay," Scarlet said. The sun glinted off her stiletto as it flashed in her hand.

Noah made a sound, more out of surprise than pain, when the blade entered his side. He slumped, and Ben caught him.

"Noah!" Ben clamped a hand on his husband's side as he lowered him onto the sidewalk. "No, no, no," he repeated as he applied pressure to the leaking wound.

"Listen, you little—" Crazy Ned, all but forgotten, grabbed Scarlet's wrist. She turned to him, and he stopped. "Your eyes! I can see that you've been touched by Hell. I'm not ready to go back!" He took a step as if to flee, not seeing Parker until it was too late. The man gave him a shove, and he fell hard against the pavement. "Stay away from me, all of you," he bellowed hoarsely as he crawled away.

"What happened?" Jackie walked up with a cup in her hand.

Scarlet's eyes fell on her and smiled.

"What did you do?" Jackie tossed the coffee to the ground and readied herself to tackle the woman. She stopped only after noticing the knife dripping with Noah's blood.

Ben grabbed her hand. "Jackie, please"—he pulled her down, pleading—"put pressure right here. Help him."

Jackie's hand replaced Ben's bloody ones as she tried to stop the bleeding. Her only focus now was helping her best friend.

"Hey, you!" Parker shouted. "Call for an ambulance!"

Ben looked up and noticed that a small crowd had gathered.

Scarlet hid her knife, and Parker started playing the innocent bystander. "That homeless guy stabbed this queer. Call an ambulance."

"Make a scene and I kill your hubby and the bitch," Scarlet whispered.

Ben looked down at Noah, who shook his head at him, telling him not to do it. The blood seeping through Jackie's fingers convinced him of what he had to do. The only option left to him, to keep them safe.

"Let's go." He peered at the crowd and spied two people talking with 911 while others recorded the scene. "Scarlet, Parker, take me to Marius, and let's finish this," he shouted, hoping their cameras picked up audio. Calling out their names might be useful later. If there was a later.

He looked down at Noah. His face was pale, the pain all too evident. Ben bent down to kiss him, but Parker grabbed him and wrenched him away with a violent jerk. "Come now, or they will need three ambulances," he growled.

"I'm sorry," Ben said, his heart breaking as Parker pulled him down the street.

Jason stood there stock-still. The whole thing unfolded in front of him so fast that he had no time to react. As sirens came closer, he looked down at Noah. Jackie glared at him, fear and anger in her eyes.

"Help me," she said, tears falling down her cheeks.

"The…the ambulance…" he stammered, watching the blood ooze between her fingers. "Shit," he swore. Throwing off his leather jacket, he stripped his black t-shirt off and handed it to Jackie. "Use this to help staunch the blood. I'll direct the EMTs here."

He ran through the crowd to flag down the ambulance.

IX

JACKIE PACED THE LIVING room, wandered into the kitchen, then back again.

Noah pretended to sleep. Since being discharged from the hospital, Jackie confined him to the couch. It hurt to lay down, but so did sitting up and standing. Luckily Scarlet had missed his major organs, though it was still a nasty wound. The blood loss made him weak, yet his mind managed to race. He replayed the entire scene in his mind: the confrontation, the stabbing, and them taking Ben away.

In the hospital, the nurses almost had to strap him down at one point. Once he regained a little strength, he climbed out of bed. He realized it was a bad idea when his head filled with stars and he almost fell to the floor. After that, Jackie refused to leave his side.

Jackie dealt with the police and the hospital staff. She gave details about the incident. The first cop grilled Noah mercilessly, trying to get him to admit that he accosted 'the defenseless white woman,' that she had been forced to defend herself. Jackie came unglued and nearly got arrested for assaulting an officer.

The next cop to show up asked questions, took statements, wished for a speedy recovery, and said she would try to find the attackers. When she left, Noah and Jackie felt no more confident that Ben would be found. Jackie even called her father, but she knew he could only do so much.

When Jackie arrived at the hospital the following day, Noah had already discharged himself. The dark circles under her eyes hinted at a lack of sleep. Noah wouldn't have been surprised if she had been searching for Ben herself. On the way home, he attempted to convince her they should do that very thing. She refused and ordered him confined to the couch for rest.

Now, tired of her pacing and the charade of sleep, he said, "Have you tried getting a hold of Jason again?"

"Yes. No answer," she said, rushing to the kitchen to get him a glass of water.

He took it, though he wasn't thirsty.

"Are you sure that's the right number?"

"It's the one he gave me when he commissioned me for the album cover. Other than an email address, I have nothing else." He sat up. "Somehow, he is caught up in this too. Maybe the whole band is. I'm guessing he knows where they took Ben."

"He might be as bad as they are." Jackie sat down.

"No, he warned us before that creepy blond guy threatened him." Noah took a drink of water to satisfy Jackie.

"That little blond prick was the creeper at the bus stop. I just now realized it. I mean, I kinda recognized him when I walked up after you got, you know… But there was so much going on," Jackie said, shaking her head. "It makes me wonder how long they've been planning this. It also makes me wonder how much they've been following us around."

"I don't know. But you need to tell the police. Do you still have that detective's card?" Noah tried to stand.

Jackie stood up, already telling him to sit back down.

"I have to take a piss." He waved her off and ambled toward the bathroom.

"I have the card, but I'm not sure it would do much to help Ben."

"Then fuck 'em," Noah called out from the bathroom. "We're going out to look for him."

"The doctor said—"

"Fuck the doctor. My husband is out there, and I will find him before these evil pricks do anything to him." Noah emerged, and the look on his face told Jackie there was nothing short of violence that would keep him from looking.

In a way, it relieved her. As much as she wanted to care for her friend, it killed her to not go out looking for Ben.

"Grab extra gauze, just in case, and your pain pills," she said, fetching her car keys. "We're going hunting."

"ARE YOU SURE HE'S not still in the hospital?" Lydia asked Jason. They both sat in the van across the street from Noah and Ben's house, waiting. "I mean, the cops are looking for you."

"I have to do something, okay?" Jason snapped at her.

She let it go. It had been a trying day already.

When Jason told them what had happened with Noah and Ben, they were all ready to pack up and leave. But he refused to go. Seeing Noah get stabbed on top of all the other shit they had witnessed spurred something in their frontman. He needed to get Ben out of Marius' clutches. Lydia understood his guilt but had no intentions of further exacerbating the situation. They had already pressed their luck enough.

That morning Jason presented them with the idea of returning to the old Victorian house, scoping things out, and retrieving the hostage if possible. Tim came along to distract Scarlet. They went over with the pretense of canceling their arrangement with Marius. As soon as they arrived, Tim and Scarlet disappeared into her room. Parker was still asleep. And Marius accepted their withdrawal with surprising aplomb. In fact, he seemed surprised they even bothered. While he and Jason talked, Lydia excused herself to 'use the bathroom' but instead went snooping for Ben.

Jason grabbed Marius' unsold merchandise from the van, giving Lydia as much time as he could. He dropped the stuff just as Lydia reappeared, giving him a knowing look.

From upstairs, Scarlet screamed. "It's in my hair, you asshole!"

Tim rushed down the stairs while zipping his pants. Scarlet's screams followed them as all three rushed out of the house. The jig was up.

Jason's next idea was to meet up with Ben's wounded husband. But he arrived right after Noah and Jackie left the house. Out of ideas, they decided to wait and think.

Tim's snoring from the rear of the van didn't help Jason's mood. Minutes went by, and he wondered if Lydia was right. Maybe they should leave town. Pack up all their shit and go.

"What if we stop, talk to the police, then go?" Jason asked. "I mean, we know where he's being held."

"Again, if we talk to the police, they will want us to stay put. And if we stay put, one of those psychos will likely kill us," Tim said groggily from the back.

"He's right," Lydia said. "I realize you want to do something, but we need to look after our own asses. Marius has washed his hands of us. That's the best position to be in."

"Anonymous tip?" Tim sat up and stretched.

"It might be the best... Wait, is that him?" Jason hopped out of the van, and the others scrambled to follow as Jackie parked her car in front of Ben and Noah's house.

"Where is he?" Noah yelled the moment he saw Jason exit the van.

He and Jackie had driven around and revisited the scene of the crime twice. They had no other leads, so they went back to the house after a couple of hours.

"I know where he is," Jason said. "But it won't be easy."

Watching Noah wince as he moved, Jason's guilt came back in waves.

"Easy means nothing to me. I just want him back." Noah leaned against the car for support.

Jackie had never seen this side of her best friend. Passionate, yes. Protective, most definitely. But he reminded her of a snake, coiled and ready to strike.

"I can show you the place, but unless you come with a bunch of cops, you'll get hurt again," Lydia informed him after catching up with the rest. "You've already seen what Scarlet can do. Parker is just as dangerous. Marius flat out doesn't care who lives or dies."

"Show us the place first," Jacking said, nodding at Noah to get back in the car. "Then we'll worry about the police."

As Noah carefully slid in, Jason told Tim to take the van back to their place and get Jake to help him pack everything up. He and Lydia then got in the back seat of Jackie's car and gave directions.

The old Victorian house sat on the city's outskirts where tradition endured as long as possible before urban renewal sunk its claws in. As usual, the urban renewal had already decayed all but the oldest structures that continued to stand tall. But even they couldn't hold back the ravages of time indefinitely.

While they sat across the street, Jackie noted more than once the severity of cliché the group operated under in the old house.

"Nothing cliché about them," Jason muttered.

"Listen, it's a full moon tonight, and the sun is already starting to go down," Lydia pointed out. "If you're calling the cops, do it now."

"You are going to back us up, right?" Jackie said, turning to the musicians and looking them in the eye.

"I…" Jason began. He looked at Lydia, then back at Jackie. "I will help you get the guy out. But after that, we're off like a prom dress. We've seen what they can do, and it's scary."

"Pants-shittingly terrifying is a better description," Lydia interjected.

"So, let's do this, and quickly."

Noah said nothing. He stared at the house as if trying to bore his vision deep past the walls to catch a glimpse of Ben. He paid little attention as Jackie dialed the police. After a few minutes of runaround, she pulled rank and mentioned her father. Redirected, they agreed to send a patrol car out.

"They won't do a thing," Noah murmured.

"I know," Jackie said, tossing the phone aside. "The patrol car is just to appease us. Without probable cause for a warrant, they'll only stare at it, the same as us."

"I'm done staring," Noah said, opening the door.

"Wait…" Jackie scrambled to follow, and the others did the same. "How do we get in unnoticed?"

The question hung in the air. Jason admitted he wasn't sure, but Lydia's heavy silence was telling.

"I guess we're really doing this," she sighed. "There is a basement window that wasn't latched last time we were downstairs."

"How did you notice that?" Jason asked, one part impressed by her observational skills and one part annoyed for furthering this insane adventure.

"Listen, I'm a female metal musician. That means I'm always surrounded by guys. Because of that, I need to be aware of every possible way out of a room. It's the reality of being a woman." She glanced at Jackie, who nodded in agreement.

"Show me," Noah ordered. Not that he didn't appreciate the sentiment she conveyed, but he had a mission, and that superseded everything else.

Lydia led the way around the side of the house, taking an educated guess where the window might be. Near the back of the house, she poked at a grimy, blacked-out window. "This is it. Wait…I hear voices."

They all stood and listened to murmuring from the room below. The voices sounded desperate. Then came the sound of feet climbing the stairs. And a door slammed.

"Sounds like they walked upstairs. Only two of them? Not sure," Jason said. "Did they do the ritual already? It's not midnight."

"Stop thinking like a poser," Lydia snapped at him. "This isn't one of your dumbass movies. Did you bother to check when the moon was full and highest in the sky? Not midnight. About an hour ago. Midnight doesn't mean shit."

"That means they might have already done something to him," Noah sobbed. Bending down to open the window, he grunted in pain.

"You are in no shape…" Jackie started.

But Noah, gritting his teeth, already had his head inside. He peered around, scanning the space.

"We don't even have a plan," Jackie continued. "Oh hell, move." She gently pushed Noah from the window. "Let me go in first, then I'll help you in."

Everything about this scared the crap out of her, but she wanted to save Ben and keep Noah from any more harm. To lose one would be devastating; to lose them both would end her.

"You want to hear the ironic part?" Jason said to Noah as Jackie shimmied through the window. "I wanted to get a hold of you to do our next album cover."

"We get Ben out and I'll do it for free."

X

THEY STOOD TOGETHER AT the base of the stairs and faced the doorway leading to the ritual room.

Lydia went pale the moment she caught a whiff of the putrid smell.

Jason wiped sweat from his forehead.

The ritual was over.

They were too late.

The door to the ritual room stood slightly ajar. Faint voices wafted out. Noah crept closer to catch the words. Without speaking to the musicians, he already guessed what they were thinking and had to push it away. If they were too late and the cult had done their little ritual, Ben might be…

"Tell me!" A voice sounded from inside the room.

Noah chanced the door. The hinges squeaked, and they all froze. But the occupant paid no attention. The group's eyes adjusted to the gloom. Several candles had gone out, yet even that didn't make the body in the room any less obvious. Noah rushed inside and collapsed to the ground next to it. In the far corner,

Parker kneeled, peering at something in the shadows. He paid the others no notice.

"Tell me, goddamn fucking demon, tell me where my cousin is. Where is Jacob? Let me speak to him." Parker's voice echoed throughout the room. Two red pinpoints of light stared back at him.

Behind him, Noah had no breath to sob. He kneeled at Ben's side, oblivious to the blood as it soaked into his jeans. Given the cuts and bruising, Ben did not go easy. Noah wanted to trace the symbols they cut into his flesh as if his touch might heal them. He watched the chest, praying for a hint of movement, a sign of lingering life. None came.

"He is deep in the Malum," a deep voice said weakly, yet it still filled the room.

All but Noah took notice. Both Lydia and Jason took a step back.

"Your dear demented cousin is situated in his self-made agony," the voice explained. "You'd be surprised the tortures he's endured so far."

"Liar. He's at the Verum Malum's right hand. I know he is. You're jealous. I want him back. Bring him back." Parker had tears of rage in his eyes. He reached into the shadows to grasp the uncooperative demon.

With sudden violence, something pushed him back. He landed hard on the floor.

"The only way you can get to your kin, you incestuous little worm, is by joining him." The demon voice weakened further, yet it still held its ground. "But I will not give you that satisfaction. You have betrayed me. You promised me a death here on Earth. Instead, you cut the ritual short. Your intention was to trap me again. Trap me between here and the Malum and leave me to die a horrible death. I will go back and face the Verum Malum, not as a demon but a tortured soul…because of you."

"Oh fuck," Jason said, surveying the scene. Something had gone seriously sideways, but he wasn't sure exactly what. He looked to Lydia. Her eyes were wide with realization and horror. He hated to admit it, but she was better at this than he was, and he suspected she had figured it out. "What did they do?"

"Marius planned on *trapping* the demon to let it die, thereby leaving a doorway open." Lydia kept her voice low as if hoping her words were only as true as their volume. "Then Ben's soul descending into the Malum would be the pathway leading Marius in."

Looking around, she saw the signs of struggle. A small metal cauldron tipped over. Blackened and congealed blood oozed out.

"Instead of coming through the body, I'm guessing they had the demon come through the blood," Lydia continued. "To come through the body would make it harder to trap. Blood is life, if still fresh. They used it instead to double-cross the demon."

Any other time she would be proud of herself for being more intelligent than the boys. Not now, though. This knowledge brought her no comfort.

"Please shut up," Jackie said, horrified at everything happening around her.

Reality threatened to buckle with the sight of Ben dead and defiled. In the shadowy corner, something else dwelled. The feeling intensified. Somehow, she knew the thing couldn't exist. Yet she knew it was there just as she knew Noah kneeled oblivious to everything but his immense and ragged grief.

Parker, getting up from the floor, noticed the visitors. "Who the fuck are you?" He peered into the gloom and recognized his audience. "Oh, you. Couldn't stay away? You should have. Excuse me for a moment. I have to finish something." He looked

Jackie in the eye, "Good to see you again, beautiful. Give me a sec. I'll be right with you."

Jackie reached down and picked up a bloodied knife from the floor.

Parker turned and approached the corner. The darkness enveloped him. Twin screams, distorted and vile, echoed through the room. An unseen struggled ensued. Then he fell out of the shadow, his head turned completely around.

"I can take some umbrage in knowing that I am bringing another one of you with me," the demon said to Parker's dead body.

"Bring him back!" Noah said, his eyes still glued to Ben's.

"Why would I do that? He was a little maggot," The demon wheezed, its end getting closer by the second.

"No! Not him! Ben. My husband. My love. Bring him back to me. Pull him from Hell, or the Malum, or whatever it is. Bring him back to me!" Noah stood and approached the demon.

The twin pricks of light were barely visible now.

"Why do you humans insist there is a way back? He is in the Malum, and he is there to stay. Shall I give him a message? I'm sure we will be side by side. Our eternity of suffering will give us plenty of time to chat."

"No, he won't. He won't suffer." Noah stood before the demon, catching some semblance of its shape before the thing dissipated. "Don't you leave me. Not until you tell me how to get to him."

"There are ways, but don't expect to come back whole," the demon said in a bare whisper. The pungent stench of sewage and rot wafted in the air. The dark corner finally gave up its shadow. The demon was gone.

"No!" Noah cried out. "You can't leave yet!"

"Afraid so," Scarlet said from the doorway. She held her stiletto casually as if weighing who to cut first. "The demon is gone, and so is your hope to get your man back. You'd be proud of him. He did a good job of jacking it all up. With Ben fighting us the entire time, it took everything we had to get the demon at all. Ben kept breaking the connections so Marius couldn't finish. Finally, we had to let both him and the demon die. It was a clusterfuck. We damn near ripped a hole to the Malum in the process. That would have been really bad." Scarlet saw Parker lying there and shook her head.

"I told him to leave that thing alone." She looked at the musicians, who were backing away from her. "You two are stupid. I'm killing you last."

"You bitch!" Noah turned to her, murder in his eyes.

Jason and Lydia moved to block his way.

Jackie stood by Ben's body as Scarlet approached her. Knife in hand, Scarlet readied to catch her as she ran.

Instead, Jackie caught her with a surprise right hook.

"Fun," Scarlet said. "You better know how to use that thing." Blood oozed from her nose as she nodded at the ceremonial knife still in Jackie's hand.

Scarlet lunged. Jackie sidestepped the blade and slashed the air, again missing Jackie.

Jackie slashed back, and Scarlet laughed at her. Then she caught her with another right, followed by an upward stab with her left, catching Scarlet right in the stomach.

Scarlet fell to her knees, eyes wide with pain.

Jackie backed away, eyes wide with the shock of what she had done.

"Fuck," Scarlet spat. "Goddamn cunt."

Jackie dropped the knife and stepped away.

No one moved. They watched Scarlet double over in pain, her life spilling onto the floor.

"Grab Ben's body," Jason said, springing into action. "We have to get out of here. The cops will arrive soon if they aren't here already. Let's go."

He took Ben by the shoulders. Noah bent to pick up his legs but howled in pain. Jackie and Lydia took his place.

"What about Marius?" Lydia asked as they navigated the stairs.

"I'll kick his goddamn face in if he tries to stop us," Jason growled.

XI

THE FOLLOWING DAYS WERE a haze of pain and despair. Noah operated only on the barest minimum. Jackie did everything she could to keep him propped up, but she had her own grief to deal with. They muddled through, supporting each other, and making arrangements. The funeral would be in two days if the police stopped dragging their feet to release Ben's body.

"I'm surprised they care." Noah slouched on the couch and tossed his phone aside. "Apparently, Marius has quite the rap sheet, so now they're suddenly concerned about what happened."

"Are they going to release Ben's body?" Jackie asked from the kitchen.

"Yes, finally. I think they are being purposely difficult," he sighed. "I need to go to the mortuary today, but I'm not sure I have the strength."

"We'll go together. Have you called Ben's parents yet?" Jackie entered with a plate of sandwiches that Noah tried to ignore. "Neither of us has eaten all day, and you didn't eat yesterday."

"Fine." He gave in and took a ham and cheese while she set the plate down, taking a turkey and swiss. "And yes, I called this morning just before you came over. They were shocked and upset. I think they were a little put out I was the one contacting them. I told them when the funeral was, but they didn't tell me if they were coming or not."

"I'm sorry, Noah. I know that wasn't an easy call," Jackie said before taking a healthy bite of her sandwich.

"Not as bad as I thought it would be. They probably won't come. Which is fine because I have no idea what a Syriac Christian funeral looks like, and I don't have the energy to argue with them. He walked away from that years ago. It would be like arguing with my parents about me having a Catholic funeral."

"Noah…"

"I'm fine. I'm just tired. And a little numb. And I hate the fact I'm numb. And I'm afraid of what will come after the numbness wears off. But I'm afraid if it doesn't wear off."

"Noah…"

"Then there's dealing with the police, who have been infuriating…"

"Noah…"

"What?"

"Eat your damn sandwich."

He looked at her. The only remnants left of her sandwich were the crumbs on her chest. He took a bite of his sandwich.

She nodded, satisfied.

AFTER A LONG AFTERNOON at the mortuary, Jackie watched Noah while he napped on the couch. He worried her. His hyper-focus on Ben's funeral caused them to argue until she sat him down and demanded he get some rest.

As exhaustion overtook him, Noah wondered aloud if he could find Marius. She assumed he wanted revenge, which mirrored her own thoughts. Instead, he shocked her by saying he wanted to find a way to bring Ben back. The creature they saw in the basement proved coming back was possible. He wanted Marius to do it again. But this time, he wanted to bring Ben back rather than summon a demon.

Ben's death overshadowed the craziness they saw in the basement. There was no denying the sight of the demon, but she wished Noah had never seen it. Once they had buried Ben, she hoped Noah might let go of this insane idea. She yawned and wondered if a nap wouldn't do her some good, too. Deciding to cover Noah first, she went to the bedroom to get a blanket from the bed. Panic slammed into her as soon as she walked in. Marius, seated on the edge of the mattress, pointed a Glock 9mm at her head.

"If you'd like to keep your brains in your skull, shut up," he said, standing.

Jackie did as she was told.

He looked pale and sweaty. His eyes twitched as he pointed at the hallway. She backed out, and he got behind her, jabbing the muzzle in her back to urge her forward. When they reached the living room, he walked past her, and she gasped. For a split second, she expected him to murder Noah right there. Instead, he raised a boot and kicked him in the ribs.

Noah howled awake and fell off the couch.

"What the fuck are you doing here?" he hollered, jumping up.

The pain in his side disappeared the moment he laid eyes on Ben's killer. He noticed the gun, but his mind, still fuzzy with sleep, took a moment to realize it was pointed at Jackie.

"I broke in while you were out," Marius said. "We have business, you and I. Now sit down, both of you."

They complied while he set down a battered black bag.

"It's a damn shame what happened at the last ritual, but it's working out in my favor. I tied up all loose ends. Parker and Scarlet were becoming a liability, and Ben's time was long overdue." Marius looked at Noah, waiting for a reaction. He received nothing but a stern glare.

"What do you want?" Jackie asked.

"I want to finish what I started. I came so close only to have the entire thing bungled." He glowered at Noah. "Despite your idiot boyfriend's best efforts."

"Husband," Noah corrected him.

"Whatever. Either way, I learned what I needed. I figured out how to reach the Verum Malum."

"You are crazy," Jackie said, sitting up.

He flashed the gun her way, and she settled back down. Hate smoldered in her eyes.

"How?" Noah asked. "How are we going there?"

Marius looked at him, a smile crossing his face. "You think you can go into the Verum Malum and save Ben, don't you? You really think you can bring him back."

"I'm going to try. He doesn't belong there. He belongs here with me."

The vehemence and conviction in Noah only made Marius smile wider.

Jackie watched the two of them, hating where this was going.

"It's your lucky day. You see"—Marius kneeled down and opened his bag—"normally, I wouldn't even consider doing something like this with the likes of you. When Ben first joined the group, he was only there because we planned to eventually sacrifice him. Or use him as a fall guy if the authorities started sniffing around. I mean, what other use is there for a dark-skinned queer?"

"Fuck you and fuck your racist, homophobic bullshit!" Noah shot out of his seat. But he stopped when Marius aimed the gun right between his eyes. His hatred radiated off him in waves.

Jackie had never known Noah to be violent, but she had no doubt, if Marius didn't have the gun, there would be violence.

"Be glad I have need of you," Marius responded. He waited for Noah to sit again before continuing to go through his bag. "It seems you will be useful to me, after all. So, for now, you get to live. It would also help you to remember that your white friend over there is only alive because I have use for her as well. If not, I'd kill her if only to teach you a lesson."

Noah and Jackie looked at each other but said nothing. Fear seeped back in and replaced much of his anger. He feared they wouldn't get out of this without someone dying.

They watched as Marius made his preparations. He moved the coffee table out of the way and marked the hardwood floor with four symbols and a large circle. He took two fat half-burnt candles and lit them, placing them at what Noah figured to be the head of the circle.

"So," Marius said as he considered his handiwork, "going to the Malum will take considerably less ceremony than you'd guess. We won't need a blood sacrifice, which is a shame because…who doesn't like a good blood sacrifice? No summoning of difficult demons or any messy rituals. All because I have a secret." He looked at the two, letting them know this was their cue to ask why.

Instead, they stared back at him in silence. He appeared even more unwell now, the anticipation making him fidget and sweat.

"I'll tell you," he continued. "It's because I got a glimpse. Ben fought us so hard that we ripped the demon through to our plane. But I got a peek of the Beyond. I'm holding that rip in my head. I've been holding it in my head the entire time. It's always there, even as I'm talking to you now. Let me tell you, it's not easy to do. So, let's begin."

Marius pointed the gun at Noah and then at the circle.

Noah stood and approached. The entire time he considered his odds of disarming the man. They weren't good, not with the pain in his side and Jackie's life in the balance.

Marius instructed him to sit.

"Don't do this, Noah. Please," Jackie pleaded.

Despite what she saw in the basement of the old Victorian, she still assumed Marius was out of his mind. She feared for their lives, but she feared for her friend's mental state too. She also feared that Marius would kill them both if they didn't succeed.

"Might I remind you that you are far more expendable than he is?" Marius said to her, sitting across from Noah in the circle. Though he put the gun in his lap, he continued to grip the handle, ready to use it if necessary. "Your job is to watch the circle. Make sure nothing interrupts us. If anything does, you will never see your friend again because he will be forever stuck in the Malum. The same goes if you try anything to me. If I die, so does he."

She saw without a doubt that he was crazy. At the first chance, she was going to stop him. She had to.

Noah stared at Marius, waiting for instruction. He was going to get Ben back. He was going to the Verum Malum to bring his husband home, and afterward, they were going to kill Marius. That was, If Jackie didn't kill him first. Noah trusted Jackie to protect him, but he hoped she would wait until he found Ben to take action. Marius might be their only way out.

"Noah, this isn't right," Jackie said, giving him her final word on the subject.

"I have to bring him back."

126

"Both of you shut up," Marius snapped. "I need to concentrate. Repeat this chant while I bring the image of the Malum forward."

He rattled off something unintelligible.

Noah had no idea what he was repeating, but it didn't really matter. He was going to retrieve Ben. Whatever the cost to his own soul, he would bring his love back to this world. Jackie didn't understand the pain. Marius didn't care. On his own in this, he had to succeed.

They continued chanting.

Marius wrote out some sigils on the hardwood in front of him. He murmured something other than the chant. With care, he withdrew a black mirror the size of a dinner plate from his bag. Placing it over the sigils, he murmured again. Once finished, he looked up at Jackie.

Instructed to stay on the couch and repeat the chant, she did as she was told, all the while leveling a deadly glare at Marius.

"Let me remind you," Marius said, "if we succeed, I'll be the only way for your fairy friend here to get out."

Jackie continued with her chanting, her gaze not wavering.

Noah stared at the black mirror. He noticed a glow of sorts coming from it. It was there yet not there. He blinked hard and returned his sight to the strange spectacle.

"Ultraviolet resonance," Marius explained, following his gaze. "It's a wavelength we can't see normally. But it's fluctuating up and down the spectrum, so our eyes are picking up the very edges of the visible wavelength. The Verum Malum is not a place we can experience with our physical senses."

"What do you mean?" Noah asked, stopping his chanting.

Marius flashed Jackie a glance, telling her to keep at it. "How else can we go there?"

Now that his hopes were up about retrieving Ben, doubts crept in. Marius might be more full of shit than he led on.

"The Malum is a place that doesn't exist in this plane. It's an entirely different dimension. Our bodies would not fit in such a place. It would be the same as if you, a 3D person, traveled to a 2D world. You would be a cross-section of yourself, just a side profile showing all your guts. To open a physical doorway there would upend all laws of physics in the immediate vicinity as they tried to exist in the same place in tandem. In a nutshell, it would be very messy. Anyone near it would die most horribly."

"So, what do we do?" Noah's fists clenched. Fear threatened his resolve. He had to get on with it before he lost all nerve.

"It's easy. Just convince your body to let go of your soul. We'll travel that way." Marius pointed at the mirror. "Keep chanting."

Long minutes passed while they chanted, the mirror's weak glow growing more intense. The illumination spread to the outer rim of the circle, enveloping the two men. Marius gasped and then whispered, "There it is."

He jerked and slumped. As he did, the mirror vibrated.

Noah kept chanting and watching the mirror. He felt a tug, not on his body but on something deeper within him. Something deeper than his mind. It tugged again. He waited for a third time, and when it came, he opened himself. Letting whatever it was inside of him, he went with it. A pain worse than anything his body had ever endured flooded him. He tried to scream, but he no longer had vocal cords. Quick as it came, the pain ended.

A profound darkness overcame him. A putrid sickness surrounded and penetrated his essence. He wanted to retch but feared he might vomit his own existence away. A heavy burning of shame, anger, sadness, and humiliation settled around him. He had worn all these emotions since Ben's death. Whatever this was, wherever he was, he wanted it to end. Even if that meant letting go of his soul.

"Stop that," said a voice that wasn't a voice. "Get a hold of yourself before you call attention to us both."

"I want it to stop. It's too much!" Noah wailed.

"I should have seen this," Marius whined. "You're weak. Get a grip!"

Noah focused on Marius' words. They were angry, tinged with desperation, and an anchor to what he had once known as 'real.' He held on to the words and tried to calm down.

"Good. Now, we'll need to work together."

"Wait, I don't see anything. I don't even see nothing. It's just, I don't know…"

Panic welled up again. Noah checked it the best he could.

"That's because we are nowhere. Think of it as the Verum Malum's front lawn. We are by all rights in the Malum, but just on the outside of it. Our beings have no context for it, so we cannot experience it with any sort of perception."

"I…"

"Don't worry about it," Marius' impatience increased. "You've heard of astral projection? Your soul traveling outside of your body? This is it, but instead of spying on your naked neighbors, we're on the outskirts of a place of pure evil and pain. Got it?"

Noah said nothing.

"I held the doorway in my mind long enough to get us here. Now we need to push through. Follow me."

He sensed Marius' 'movements' and followed. The whole experience disoriented him because the movements had no sense of direction. No forward or backward, only passage through an empty geometry.

"What was that?" Noah blurted out as everything around them contracted and expanded. It happened once more before a sudden brightness blinded him.

"Welcome to the Malum," Marius said as Noah's sight returned.

XII

A SICK, BLEAK LANDSCAPE spread before them. The mottled red sky bathed everything in a bloody hue. Bare and twisted trees rose from brown earth, barren and diseased. A row of squat buildings made of gray blocks crouched upon the terrain. In the far distance, a mountain range looked painted onto the skyline.

"This isn't what I expected," Noah said after taking it all in. He expected fire and brimstone, frozen wastes, heads on pikes, or a mind-wasting series of interdimensional vertices. Instead, they stood on a stone platform in a vaguely familiar village. Why it looked familiar, he couldn't say.

"I am underwhelmed." Marius looked around before climbing down from the platform. It appeared to be made of the same rectangular stone as the buildings. "Everything is so boxy-looking…almost like it's…"

"Pixilated," Noah finished for him, realizing why it looked familiar. "There was a video game, way back in the day, in which you wound up going to Hell and had to fight your way through demons and whatever else. I played it when I was a kid. I loved that game."

"Oh, I get it," Marius said, looking up to the sky and laughing. "Very cute. A nice touch." He turned back to Noah, who seemed confused. "This place doesn't exist in a way that can be associated with our reality. We are here only in spirit, literally. But as spirit, we still need to process it somehow. Our bodies and minds normally do the processing, so we will see this place based only on how we can understand it. Therefore, our minds will use our general idea of 'Hell' to ease us into it. Understand?"

"I get what you mean…sort of. So, I see Hell as a mid-90s video game for some reason. That part I don't fully understand."

"To be honest, neither do I," Marius said in a sniffy way while slowly walking toward the first building. "I've seen your work, and it's good. Even the cover you did for that idiotic metal band. From your mind, I would expect something darker and more, I don't know, Catholic."

Noah caught up with him, remembering why he hated the man. He also noticed that his knife wound no longer hurt. "You're such a bigot that your idea of Hell is an eternity with people like me."

Marius peered into the window of the first building. It had no glass, only a boxy chair and a cold boxy fireplace. "It wouldn't be the ultimate torture, but it would rate right up there."

"I don't need you. I'm going to find my husband." Noah turned and walked away, heading up the short lane.

"How do you plan on doing that?" Marius hollered. "I've spent my life studying the incomprehensible, the seemingly intangible. I understand more about the Verum Malum than any one person. I'd stick close if I were you. Anything happens to me, you're stuck here forever."

He turned and walked with a brisk gait toward the farthest building.

Swearing, Noah followed.

"We came together, so you need me just as much," he called after him.

"Yes, but for other reasons," Marius said over his shoulder. He walked past the last building, identical to the others, and stopped at one of the short, sick trees. He grabbed it with his hand and pulled hard. It moved, opening like a secret door. A perfect rectangle appeared as if the doorway existed in the very air itself. "Remember that nothing is as it seems here."

They both walked into a massive room, dark as night and nearly as big. A vaulted ceiling loomed unseen over their heads. The walls held flickering candles on dangerous-looking sconces, their light almost too far away to do much good. Rows and rows of pews surrounded them, interrupted by an occasional large stone cistern full of fresh red blood. Ahead of them, large illuminated stained glass sat behind an altar of sorts. Fortunately, it was too far away for Noah to make out much detail.

"I assume this is your idea of Hell, then?" Noah asked Marius as they walked.

"Better than yours, isn't it? I always loved the idea of a Black Mass. The perversions of what you Eucharist-eaters hold so dear. Why wouldn't the Devil want his own church?"

"I'm not Catholic anymore. The pope is still all wishy-washy on us 'homos.' And besides, you said this wasn't Hell but something worse," Noah grumbled.

"Oh, it is. But I had to change it into something less embarrassing."

They walked on, saying nothing else for a while. The church seemed a mile long. Noah made out some of the designs as they neared the stained glass. Most of them were the same symbols used to bring them here. There were other things, too. Scenes of bloody murder, decapitations, castrations, female mutilations, and rape spread around the symbols. If Marius was right, he built this place from his subconscious, and Noah was getting a deeper look at it than he wanted.

"I expected to see other things. Where are the demons?" Noah asked, realizing they hadn't come across any other living creature since they arrived.

By way of reply, Marius pointed a finger up.

Noah followed the indicating digit and noticed black movement above the candlelight.

"Demons. They are not happy that we are here. But they dare not do anything to us. They used to be human, and the only way they can escape is to find a way back. To piggyback on us would be a way home to die in peace."

Noah peered into the surrounding darkness to see what else lurked in the gloom. The demons moved around in an agitated mass while keeping their distance. He strained to see what they looked like. Then again, he wasn't sure he wanted to.

Once they reached the altar, Marius beamed at the massive stone structure, behind which only a giant could stand. Noah assumed Marius would envision his Devil to be so large. But on further reflection, this wasn't for any devil. Marius would stand behind it, the giant of a man he envisioned himself to be. Noah felt dirty walking around in this madman's ego.

A doorway opened to their right, leading somewhere much brighter than the dark cathedral.

"Shame. I wanted to explore this a little more."

"I'm not here to be a tourist. C'mon," Noah said, already heading toward the doorway regardless of what he might encounter. He came for Ben, not to stand around gawking.

Marius followed at a more leisurely pace.

The contrast of the brighter light and the dark cathedral left Noah blinded as he stepped through the doorway.

"Oh god!" Noah gagged. His feet sank into something soft and wet. Looking down, he found himself ankle-deep in intestine. The entire floor was a swamp of entrails.

"Whew, that is rank," Marius whistled, raising his arm to his nose. "But this is more like it."

Intestine and bowel lined the entire room, floor to ceiling. Tall square pillars stood, ten to a side. In the center of each hung a person. A large chain entered their rectums, ran through their insides, and came out of their mouths. Bellies cut open, their guts cascaded down their fronts, and the wet chains gleamed in the cavities like metal spines.

"Are...are they alive?" Noah asked, watching their small movements.

"I'm guessing so." Marius betrayed a small amount of glee.

Noah bent over and threw up.

"Is this you again? Because this didn't come from me," he said as he wiped his mouth.

"No. I appreciate the style, but this is the Malum proper. These are souls being tortured."

"By the Verum Malum, correct? Ben explained it, but I'm still a little fuzzy on the details," Noah said, walking forward with tentative steps, trying not to puke again.

"The Verum Malum governs this place, the Malum. He is beyond religion and even God. He might even be the true essence of the universe," Marius said, walking past Noah to the next door.

"Same shit, different names," Noah murmured, taking one more look at the disemboweled souls before following Marius through to an opposite doorway.

They did not enter a room but a vast landscape where a foul wind gusted. A roughhewn path wound down a canyon wall. Outcroppings here and there contained more souls experiencing tortures that neither man immediately discerned. At the bottom of the canyon, black water flowed. Noah looked up the path and saw they weren't too far from the top. Wanting a better view, he hiked up, ignoring Marius' warnings against it.

Just after the edge of the canyon, a long fence stretched beyond his vision. He peered at it and realized the slats and posts of the fence were pulsing. What he took as a knothole turned out to be an eyeball looking at him, pleading with him. Noah quickly trotted back down the path. Whatever a fence like that kept at bay, he did not wish to know.

Marius had already started down the path, so Noah was forced to catch up with him. They made it to the first outcropping. On it stood a man nailed to a rock.

The victim watched them go, his chin high and eyes proud. His gaze dared them to say anything. Once out of earshot, Marius whispered, "He seems proud of his station."

"Yeah," Noah agreed.

Some people were masochists, but he never dreamed to this level. People weren't that into their own pain, were they?

The further they walked, the more they saw variations of the same thing: people impaled, scarred, disemboweled, or continuously lighting themselves on fire. All of them silent, stoic, with an eerie sense of pride. On the last outcropping stood a woman cutting her own head off with a blade. The head tumbled to the ground and rolled to the edge, and the body caught it right before it fell. Clumsy hands set it back on the stump, and the wound immediately healed. Without hesitation, she took the blade and hacked away at her neck again until her head fell off and nearly rolled over the edge.

"Why, though?" Noah asked out loud as they passed by.

His voice startled the woman, causing the body to hesitate for a split second. That was all it took for the hands to fumble the head. It went over the edge and fell, screaming until it splashed into the dark water. Her jarring screams were the first sounds any of these souls had made since they had arrived.

The path turned away from the water and led into a large cave. Horror littered the inside of the space. They stepped around it with extreme care. The cacophony of sounds emanating from the darkness made him wish for the eerie silence again.

He tripped over a man being shat out of a woman. The man cried and attempted to scramble away. But the woman threw him to the ground and cuddled him like a mother. She held him so tightly that he couldn't move or breathe. His head to her breast, she pulled him right through her skin, and he disappeared inside of her. After a moment, she sounded a thunderous fart and shat him out again. And the appalling cycle continued, agonizingly, endlessly.

Around a corner, they came across a man sitting at a fire. Laid over the flames was an assortment of small rods. Across from the fire, several impish children danced naked. The man's obvious erection betrayed his wicked desire. The children danced and laughed, and the man laughed with them until two large black hands reached out and gripped his shoulders from behind. As the dark demonic shape held him in place, the man's laughter died. Each of the imp children took a glowing rod from the fire and held it between their fingers. Noah cringed at the man's screams and the sizzling as they inserted the first rod into his urethra.

"Holy shit," Noah whispered.

Marius said nothing. He laughed at a few of the tortures they came across, but some were too much, and even he had to look away. Like the man being consumed by flies and a homophobic rape.

Noah assumed that might be a little too close to an actual Hell for Marius. For just a moment, he imagined the poor bastard being spared the demon's fence-post-sized phallus and pictured Marius in his place. He shook the image away. No matter how badly he wanted Marius dead, and no matter how much Marius deserved an eternity here, Noah had to fight to keep this place from affecting him. He had to focus on Ben.

"Do you know where you're going?" Noah asked, realizing they had no sense of destination.

"The only way we can go. I haven't noticed any other roads, have you?" Marius asked, skirting a scattered jigsaw puzzle of a human. The disassembled person managed to click another piece of its leg into place when there approached a giant wheel made of five people. Their heads had been fitted up each other's rectums to keep it together. Rolling, the wheel of flesh and bone gained momentum until it crashed into him, scattering the pieces all over again. A hand fell at Noah's feet. He grabbed it and set it into a nearby arm piece.

Marius harrumphed.

The end of the horror cave neared. At the exit stood the silhouette of a man. It didn't look like another of the tortured. In fact, it seemed to be waiting for them. As they neared, Noah recognized some features but held back any excitement. This is not the place for hope, he reminded himself. But as they got closer, there was no mistaking who stood there.

"Isn't this fucking convenient?" Marius scowled as Noah broke into a run and flung his arms around the man.

"Ben! I found you! Oh my god! I was beginning to think I never would!"

Noah held him tight, tears springing from his eyes. The farther into the cave they had traveled, the farther away the hope of finding him had faded. But here he was, in his arms at last. Noah squeezed him even tighter.

Ben leaned into Noah and whispered in his ear three heartbreaking, dread-inducing words: "I'm not Ben."

XIII

JACKIE SAT PENSIVE ON the couch. She stared at the two men sitting on the floor. Their bodies slumped, showing no signs of life besides their breathing. She couldn't bring herself to breach the strange light surrounding them. Faint noises and smells wafted from the circle here and there, but they were too fleeting for her to recognize. She remained vigilant. Marius had told her to guard them, so that's what she was doing.

Guard them against what? she wondered.

Time crawled.

The light outside grew dim, and she had a powerful need to use the bathroom. But she dared not move. If she saw any signs of life, she would pull Noah out of the circle. She contemplated doing it numerous times already but feared what might happen if she did. Doubt and confusion were her only active companions. She never once gave credence to an afterlife. Yet watching the men and the odd colors and sounds, she realized their souls were no longer in their bodies. Belief in the concept of a soul was new to her as of this afternoon, but she'd cross one bridge at a time. As much as she feared hurting Noah, she feared doing nothing would too.

Deep in her train of thought, she tried to imagine where they might be. That's when someone knocked on the front door, and she screamed. She shot to her feet, nearly falling from the pins and needles in her legs. She flung the door open to find all four members of Emaciated Angel on the doorstep.

"What's wrong?" Lydia asked. "You look like you saw a ghost."

Jackie had no words available, so she opened the door wider, revealing Marius and Noah in the circle.

"Well, shit," Tim said from over Jason's shoulder.

The group entered the house and surrounded the circle. They started talking amongst themselves about the scene, what rite Marius might have used, the possibilities of actually being in the Malum, and so forth.

Jackie watched them for a few moments before yelling, "What's going on here?"

They all turned to her.

"Listen," she said, "I get it. There is some 'magical' rite, and they went to some horrible afterworld. But there is still so much I don't understand, so much I didn't want to understand. Not until we found Marius in the house and he forced us to do this."

"What a bastard," Jason said, eyes still on the circle.

"What do I do? That's what I want to know. I'm supposed to be guarding them. But why am I am guarding them? And from what?" Jackie sat back down on the couch, grateful that someone else had come.

Jake sat down on the other end of the couch, his face screwed up in concentration.

"Well," he said, "I'll admit that I don't understand as much about this stuff as the rest. And to be honest, I'm just into it because it sounded cool and got me laid. But your best course of action would be to take that gun in Marius' lap, put it to his head, and pull the trigger."

"I've been leaning toward that as a strong option," she admitted, "but he claims to be Noah's only way out."

"You honestly expect Marius to help him?" Lydia asked, giving Marius's shoulder a nudge with her boot.

Jackie sat up with a curious expression.

Lydia had breached the circle, and nothing happened.

Jackie stood up again and took the gun from Marius' limp hand. She looked at the weapon and then at him. She thought about it, shaking her head. It was too risky.

"Jesus, Tim. Really?" Jason's exclamation broke her thoughts. She looked up to see Tim coming out of the kitchen, an overflowing sandwich in his hand.

"What? I haven't eaten yet today. Not like he'll mind." He nodded at Noah.

Jason glared and pointed at Jackie.

"You don't mind, do you?" Tim asked, realizing his faux pas.

"No. Do you mind making me one?" Jackie asked, exhausted down to her soul. "I haven't eaten yet, either."

NOAH STOOD IN SHOCK, something he didn't believe possible anymore. The man that stood in front of him looked like Ben in every way. His short black hair, stubbled jawline, and broad shoulders were all the same. Only the eyes were different. Something glowed behind them.

"I am not Ben," the deep gravelly voice said again.

"Where is he? Why do you look like him?"

"You misunderstand me. I am not Ben, but this is Ben. I am taking his soul for a brief ride, so to speak," he said, increasing Noah's confusion and anxiety.

"You…you are the Verum Malum…" Marius said in awe.

'Ben' nodded.

"How…I mean…how can you be in a soul? That's like two objects being in the same point in space. It's not possible."

"Because we are in *this* place, and I AM this place," the Malum explained. "As for why I am inside your friend, I figured I'd come meet you in a form you'd recognize."

"Is my husband okay?" Noah asked, still trying to get a grasp on this information. "Is he in pain right now?"

"He is very far from okay." The Malum smiled.

"Can we see your true form?" Marius took a place next to Noah.

Noah noticed that his entire attitude had changed. No longer the smug psychopath, he acted like a schoolboy asking his favorite teacher a question.

"You would not be able to withstand the sight of it. Remaining tethered to your bodies puts you in an in-between state. You are not spirit, but you are not physical either. There are many things you are not able to handle if I should show them to you." The Malum spread his arms to indicate their surroundings. "Look around you and see me as this, for it is who I am as well."

Marius nodded at the information.

Noah found himself struggling with it. He said nothing, though. Instead, he fought back the surge of hopelessness that threatened to overtake him. How could he separate Ben from this ultimate evil? And if he did, how would he get them both back home?

Marius peppered the Malum with questions, but Noah paid little mind. The Malum did the same. The expression of mild amusement slid from its face, and it merely stood there waiting for Marius to pause. Then one question caught both Noah and the Malum's attention.

"So, the Verum Malum is a gigantic cave?"

"No, it is not. This is an entryway. One of countless such access points. In fact, the only reason these souls are here is because of their impatience to begin their torture. So invested in their own torments, they stopped short and commenced to their business." The Malum shrugged.

"So, you don't torture people? They do it themselves?" Noah asked. Though he had seen plenty nightmarish acts thus far, he still didn't want to admit it.

"I do plenty to them, but most of the work they do themselves. The demons help where needed. Come." It turned and walked out of the cave.

The three of them walked into something vaster than the night sky. Comprised of pitch black and blinding light simultaneously, it expanded forever. Noah picked out odd geometries and movements. As he focused, he realized he saw activity all around them. Like standing in a skyscraper and seeing through all the walls, he watched different layers of the Verum Malum at the same moment. In these layers, people were in pain and undergoing torture, others alone and miserable, some packed in so tightly they couldn't move. Demons, their ink-black bodies peppered throughout these layers, performed horrible tasks.

"This is, as you would call it, the Verum Malum. This is me," the Malum said, watching their faces, relishing their reactions.

"We call you Verum Malum, yes, but what is your true name?" Marius asked, his face full of awe and wonder at the eternal horror around him.

"You don't fool me. You think if you get my 'true name,' you can gain power over me. I see through you, little human. What use do I have for a name?"

Marius dropped the pretenses of being the awestruck visitor. The smug know-it-all returned. He shrugged at being called out. "Can't blame me for trying."

Noah couldn't take his eyes away from everything going on around him. Like driving by the scene of an accident, his eyes refused to look away. Only this time, he was driving by an infinity of accidents. Endless traumas. Watching the demons reminded him of the infernal presence they encountered in the basement where they found Ben. That demon wanted to die on Earth. An idea came to him.

"What are the demons? Do you make them?" Noah asked, unable to look directly at the Malum. Seeing Ben's form and knowing he was in there somewhere, undoubtedly enduring some unimaginable pain, killed Noah inside.

"The demons are more or less self-appointed. They do whatever dirty work the denizens don't do to themselves. Plus, with so many souls, someone needs to do the caretaking. Pruning the hedges and spraying down the walk, so to speak."

"Then what do you do?"

"I exist. Before you humans came to me, I simply existed as I am. It was only when you arrived that I realized the concept of 'doing.'" The Malum turned to Marius. "That is why I have no 'true name.' Why would a single entity need a name? Besides, when you souls arrived, you already had so many other names on your lips."

"Still can't get used to the idea that you are both a person and a place," Noah mumbled.

"Whether you can or cannot is of no consequence to me," the Malum said dismissively.

He turned away, and their surroundings changed from the vast sky of torture to a tall chamber with walls of mottled flesh and large pulsating pillars. Ahead of them, a platform raised up. A throne made of confusing geometries rose with it. The Malum sat and faced them.

The time for questions had ended. Marius clearly knew this. Noah sensed that he was up to something. Something that would potentially leave both he and Ben stuck here. But Marius wasn't as clever as he fancied himself, which concerned Noah even more, as he might doom them both with his ambition. He tried to concentrate on a plan.

"I want to be your agent on Earth," Marius blurted, getting to the point. "Bestow me with powers, and I will do your bidding. I can bring you more souls or—"

The Malum's laughter cut off Marius' entreaties and unnerved Noah. It reminded him too much of Ben's laugh.

"Why would I care about what goes on *there*? I don't need more souls! I don't invite any of you, but still, you come. There isn't some cosmic karmic law that ferries them to me. You come, and I accommodate. And be glad I do. If you had to deal with your own self-damning souls, your fragile little species would have extinguished itself millennia ago."

"Or we would have learned more about our true natures," Noah said with an edge of defiance.

"Your optimism is comically naïve. As for you"—the Malum turned to Marius again—"I know exactly what you want. It is written all over you. You want power, and you have no intention of doing anyone's bidding but your own. Even if I could somehow give you power over your fellow humans, it would be of no advantage to me."

"But I can—"

"Enough. I am already tired of this," the Malum cut him off again. "The two of you have trespassed too long. The fact that you are still tethered to your own plane is problem enough, let alone your incessant questions."

"Being tethered to our own plane is a problem?" Marius asked.

But the Malum didn't take the bait.

"Have others trespassed?" Noah asked, remembering Crazy Ned's stories. He needed to buy a little more time.

"Oh yes. But none of them returned whole." Though the Malum answered Noah, his eyes never left Marius. "Now, my little maniac, it's time I deal with you. It might please you to find out that you are quite famous here. I've been aware of your attempts to reach me, and many of the demons have whispered your name. They think your mucking around will leave them a doorway to escape. But they are also lined up to cause you oceans of pain for what you did to their own."

Both Noah and Marius looked over their shoulders. A mass of black entities stood behind them. Their glowing red eyes all fixed on Marius. Noah experienced their intentions like a wave of heat. He took a step away.

Marius looked at them and back at the Malum. Any pretense dropped away, and he began pleading with both the demons and the Malum.

Noah put more distance between himself and Marius. He didn't know what would happen, but he knew it wouldn't be good.

The Malum spoke something that Noah felt more than he heard. It was more than language, yet less than a word. A demon walked out of the crowd. No matter how hard he tried, he still couldn't get a good look at the forms of these entities. So many things here looked clear and yet hard to see. Maybe because he wasn't just a soul here but a spiritual projection. A piece of soul stretched into the wasteland.

"That's precisely what it is," the Malum said.

To Noah's horror, he realized his thoughts were being read.

"Oh yes," the Malum said, "I sense your thoughts. And I know your plans. You wonder if you can convince me to make your mate a demon so you can somehow take that demon back home. Even have it possess a body. Am I right?"

Noah nodded, defeated.

"You're an idiot." Marius turned on Noah with venom. "You'll doom us both with your idiocy."

"It was your body he was hoping to have possessed," the Malum revealed. "But it will already be occupied."

Again, the Malum said the odd name. Before Marius could react, he froze in rigid pain. Behind him, the demon raised a sharp hand that dripped strings of slick crimson. It then rotated Marius's body to show a cut up the back, asshole to head. A cut so deep and precise that Noah could see marks in the spinal column and severed nerves. The demon peeled the skin off the body with expert care, like stripping a suit from a mannequin. At that point, Marius found his voice box, and his screams caused Noah to press his hands over his ears.

Completely skinned, Marius' raw body fell to the ground. Guts spilling out, he struggled to pull them back in with feeble hands while his screams died to mewling whimpers.

To Noah's horror, he watched the demon put the skin on and wear it like a suit of its own. Through the eyeholes, the demon's red glowing eyes looked at him. With its wretched features now fitted into the spiritual form tethered to Marius' earthly body, a wicked smile formed on the creature's face.

"What will happen to him?" Noah turned to the Malum, forcing himself to look at it.

"Oh, this is a good one. I can rarely scoop a soul out of a physical body. Your friend here is being tortured here *and* on Earth. I've spiritually disemboweled him and left his actual body an empty husk. But as you can see, someone else now wears his 'skin.' Back on Earth, my demon will wear the skin too. It will wreak some havoc, probably kill your body, and come back home."

"But...he was my ride," Noah blurted, remembering the first time he met Marius. From that moment, his life became hell and resulted in the loss of his love.

Now possibly an eternity here. With nothing left to lose, he looked the Malum in its glowing eyes.

"I want to talk to my husband."

XIV

"OKAY, UNPOPULAR OPINION—WHAT IF they aren't in the Malum but in a trance?" Jake asked, getting restless.

"How do you explain the odd energy surrounding the circle?" Jackie said. "Plus, I saw something. When they crossed over, or whatever you call it, I caught a glimpse of where they went."

Jake had nothing to say after that.

Jackie stood guard over the circle as the group sat around the living room. There weren't many available options despite the many ideas they traded back and forth.

Jason and Lydia, the two who had closely studied the rituals of Marius and Alexander, wracked their brains trying to come up with a way to bring Noah back. Tim and Jake gave less helpful suggestions while Jackie watched the two men in the circle, waiting for any changes. She tried desperately to maintain a practical outlook to keep from losing her mind.

"It doesn't matter if this is all absolute madness," she told them. "It's happening whether I believe it or not."

Marius' body twitched, and the air in the room shifted. Everyone became quiet and watched the circle. The faint energies around it thickened for a moment. Jackie held the gun tight in her hand.

"Please, Noah," she whispered. But his body sat still while Marius' spasmed.

The body shifted again. His shoulders rounded, and he stretched his neck.

Jackie raised the Glock and pointed it at the back of Marius's head. Her eyes jogged back and forth between Marius and Noah. Her best friend still did not move.

"Um…" Tim fell into a crouch, ready to run. His eyes widened. "Jason, am I seeing…"

"Oh no," Jason said as he backed away from the circle.

Marius' head turned to face Jackie. The eyes that stared at her were not his. They burned a bright red, glowing like embers, radiating hate and malice.

"Hello, friends," said a deep voice that resonated in their chests.

Jackie didn't realize she had pulled the trigger until after Marius' body flew back and sprawled on the ground. A deep choking scream faded away, and blood began pooling into the floorboards.

"Holy shit! Demonic possession!" Jake exclaimed, half excited, half scared.

No one else moved.

Jackie turned her attention from the dead body to Noah. No change.

"What do we do now?" Lydia asked. She looked to Jason, then to Jackie.

Jackie put the gun down on the table and took a shaky breath. Then another less shaky one. "Lydia, go into the bathroom and bring me some towels. Tim and Jake, sit the body up to keep more blood from draining out. Jason, we will need a tarp."

"Um…" Jason hesitated.

"Listen," Jackie snapped at him, "we now have a dead body and a huge mess. We need to get rid of both and quickly. This isn't the type of neighborhood used to hearing gunfire. The last thing we need is neighbors seeing all this."

By the time she finished talking, Lydia already had an armload of towels. Tim and Jake sprang into action and hauled Marius's body into a sitting position, trying not to get blood on their clothes. Jason slid out the front door in search of a tarp.

"Jam towels in the gaping hole in his head. We'll worry about cleaning up after we get rid of the body," Jackie instructed. She peeked out the window to see if anyone in the neighborhood had emerged to investigate. No one so far. Either they hadn't heard the gunshot or assumed it was fireworks. "Good. We'll wrap the body in the tarp and put it in the tub. Once Noah gets back, we'll head out of town toward the Flats. It'll be a good place to hide the body."

"I'm afraid to ask, but how do you know all this?" Tim asked as he held the body upright, still trying not to get blood on his hands.

"A lifetime of detective stories over the dinner table," Jackie said, her attention going back to Noah.

Tim mimicked his lead guitarist's voice: "*We'll stop in for a minute and pay our condolences*, Jason says. *Then we'll get tacos and leave town*, he says."

NOAH WATCHED THE MALUM as it considered his request. He took this as a hopeful sign. The longer he spent here, the worse things became. A barrage of images danced in his mind. Faint pictures of Ben and Marius having sex started it. He imagined himself surrounded by empty liquor bottles, his friends and family pissing on him in anger. Despair crept in.

Memories of dead pets and other painful experiences paraded around him, a continuous projection of his worst moments. He tried his best to push it all away, but the longer he stayed here, the worse it became. Whether intentionally designed for it or not, the Verum Malum encouraged personal pain with extraordinary glee.

"He stays here," the Malum said after some contemplation. "He pledged himself to me, and while I don't care a whit about that type of thing, I hate to disappoint his expectations. And it's poor policy to let souls leave simply because they want to."

"You'll let me speak to him then?" Noah asked. The idea of seeing Ben again, the real Ben, wiped away all the darkness that threatened to envelop him.

"Yes, for a few moments, but you can't take him back. Like I said, I know your plans." The Malum stood and approached him. "Once you've said your goodbyes, you must leave. This has been a nice little distraction, but I'm over it. The fact that you are here and in your own world simultaneously is too much of a strain. The longer you remain, the thinner the barriers become. Easier to just let you go home. Unless you don't have a body to go home to. Then I can arrange something."

Noah prayed the demon wearing the Marius skin didn't hurt anyone or cause him to be stuck here forever.

The congregation of demons behind him grew restless. He turned to see a demon standing next to him. It addressed its master. "They reacted quicker than expected."

Despite all the demons looking the same to him, Noah recognized it as the one that had put on Marius' skin.

"Is Jackie okay? Did you hurt her?" Noah yelled at the creature.

It focused its burning eyes on him. "Quite the quick draw she was. One bullet to the head." The demon looked down at Marius' skinned body, still huddled on the floor, then raised its eyes to the Verum Malum. "Shall we take him away?"

"Yes. In fact, we'll do something a little extra for him. His greatest wish was to come and meet me. Let's put him back on that quest again. It seemed to make him so happy. But make sure he never quite gets here. I will always one step away, just beyond his reach. And your demons can torment him all you like. That will be a proper setup for the likes of him."

The demons picked up Marius.

He screamed with every movement.

"You're sending him back to Earth?" Noah asked.

"Oh no. He'll believe he is. Obsessives are easy. Dangle the carrot but never let them catch it."

"Make sure it's a world full of people of color and the queer community," Noah suggested, unable to help himself.

The Malum nodded. "I like the way you think. You would do well here."

"Give Ben back to me," Noah demanded, refusing to be denied or distracted from the reason he had come all this way.

The Malum held out a hand.

With trepidation, Noah reached out and took it.

The amused expression slid from Ben's face to be replaced by one of pain, then relief. The glowing of his eyes faded out, and Noah knew he was looking at his love. A blinding light erupted behind Ben, but Noah's only focus was his husband. Ben pulled him into a tight hug. Tears sprang into both of their eyes.

"Noah," Ben whispered.

Noah snuggled in tighter, determined to never let him go.

"Noah, whatever you do, don't look behind me."

"I only want to see you, nothing else," Noah said into his shoulder.

"I'm serious." Ben pulled him away and held his head so that he only saw his face. "You are still attached to your body. Behind me is what that evil bastard really looks like, and you can't handle seeing it. It will break you."

"You're all I want to see," Noah said and kissed him deeply.

Ben responded in kind, and they melted into each other again. The kiss lasted both an eternity and a second.

"How bad is it?" Noah asked when they parted.

"Sharing a soul with him is like always drowning but never dying. Instead of water filling you up, it's knife blades. Love, you have to go now," Ben said, still keeping Noah from moving his head and peeking at the evil entity.

A voice surrounded them yet came from nowhere. It boomed, "You've had your time. If you have any hope of going home, now is it. Otherwise, plan on an eternal stay."

"He means it." Ben held Noah tight, burying Noah's head in his shoulder. "He doesn't care whether you stay or go, but it's easier for him that you leave. The boundary between the planes is open, and it hurts him. It closes quicker if you go home, but all he cares about is that it closes."

"I have no way back home. Marius is dead."

"You are still attached to your body. Imagine a silver cord that stretches through an empty eternity and leads back home. Your soul and body are still linked, and home is your body. Concentrate on your home," Ben whispered once, then whispered it again.

As he concentrated, Noah felt what Ben was talking about. He could feel the cord attached to his back. He followed that cord, sensing the home of his body. It was fleeting, though, and he grasped to hold on to it. His concentration would only hold out so long.

"That's enough. Give me back what is mine," the Malum boomed.

With a rough jerk, Ben was snatched from Noah's arms.

"No!" Noah yelled.

There came a tug from the cord. Now that he had a way back home, his survival instincts were pulling him back. As he parted from Ben, his heart wrenched at the thought of losing him again. He wouldn't be able to live knowing Ben would spend eternity in this place. Straining against his own will to go home, he pushed forward, away from his body. Reaching out, he took his husband's hand, surprising both Ben and the Malum. Noah pulled him into his arms, holding tighter than he had held anything before. He let the cord snap them backward and away.

Head on Ben's shoulder, he opened his eyes and chanced a look at the Malum. It was only a fraction of a second, but it was too late. He saw a dark wall that was also a face. The eyes and mouth were open wide with a blinding light bursting from them. Noah understood it wasn't the real Malum, just his brain trying to understand what it really saw. Even that was too much, though, as the image tried to shift to its true nature.

He saw that true nature for an even briefer instant, and that was all it took. The image went black, the visual relief cut short from a searing pain in both eyes. Noah tried to open his lids to see and realized his eyes were already open. Still, he saw nothing.

"My love," Ben said in a sob, "I warned you."

Ahead, they heard Jackie's familiar voice scream Noah's name. A cloud of demons had given chase, but they soon fell away, unable to catch up.

The Malum chuckled in the distance.

Noah slammed back into his body, jarring him physically and spiritually, leaving him with a heavy queasy feeling. He wanted to throw up, but that required him to get reacquainted with his internal organs again. Other matters were more pressing.

"Ben!" he screamed.

Five others screamed in surprise.

Noah still saw nothing, but he smelled an odor of burned flesh and blood.

"Ben!" he yelled again.

"I am here…for a moment," Ben's wispy voice said. "You saved me. My spirit is no longer tied to the Verum Malum. Thank you, my love."

"Ben?" Jackie said.

Noah heard the tears in her voice.

"Take care of him, please," Ben said, the voice fading.

"I always do," Jackie sobbed.

Noah called out for him again but got no answer.

"He's gone."

Noah put his hand to the floor to steady himself, and it landed in a slick, wet spot. "What the…?"

"That's blood," Lydia said. "Hold on, I'll see if there is another towel."

He wiped his hand on his pants and touched his face with his other hand.

"What is this?"

He felt charred flesh around his eye sockets.

"I don't know what happened," Jason admitted. "You were just sitting there, then you screamed, and your eyes…they burned without any sign of fire. Just sizzled away."

"You don't have any eyes," another voice said, both horrified and fascinated. "The sockets are empty."

171

"Who is all here, and where is Marius? Did the demon hurt anybody?" Noah clumsily tried to stand.

Hands grabbed him and guided him to the couch.

"Jason and the rest of the band are here. They helped me," Jackie said. "The demon is dead. I shot it in the head after it possessed Marius. We've got it handled." She pulled him close and held him.

Noah wanted to cry, wanted to feel hot tears on his face. He couldn't even do that now.

"I saved Ben. It was worth the cost," he said, pulling away.

Jackie still held on to him. "Yes, you did. I don't get how, but you did."

"Um, I don't want to break up the moment, but we should do something about this body," Tim said. "I'm really tired of keeping it from bleeding on your floor."

"Yeah, sorry about the crime scene in your living room," Jason said, the rustle of plastic crinkling about the room. "But at least we have a tarp now."

"Are you taking the body out to the Flats?" Noah asked Jackie.

"No place better," Jackie kissed him on the forehead, her tears falling on him.

"I'll drive," Noah said with a weak laugh that turned into a sob, and he cried in joy and loss, both emotions more intense than he ever thought possible.

ABOUT THE AUTHOR

Mick Collins was born at a very young age in the wilds of southern Idaho. After a few decades, he finally got his fill of all the sagebrush and rattlesnakes he could eat, so he struck out into the world. After some time in Texas and Pennsylvania, he currently is currently back Idaho with his partner Mel. He is a Bi author who has published a number of novels and short stories. His most recent books are Verum Malum and Night Shall Overtake (as Michael R. Collins), and Dick Wiggler and Other Useless Superpowers (writing as Mick Collins) as well as penning a few alibis. (Just in case)

https://michaelrcollins.wordpress.com/

https://linktr.ee/mrcollins

https://godless.com/collections/michael-r-collins

ACKNOWLEDGMENTS

SMALL STORY, BUT BIG thanks, to Nick White, Kathleen Kapila, and Jason Gehlert for your beta reading expertise. Also, a big thanks to James Carlson at Gloom House for taking a chance on this infernal little tale. And to the love of my life, Mel, for the constant inspiration and endless patience.

Also By Uncomfortably Dark Horror

ANTHOLOGIES

Uncomfortably Dark presents The Baker's Dozen-2021 Dark Dozen anthology & the 2022 Splatterpunk award-winning extreme horror anthology.

Uncomfortably Dark presents Trapped-2022 Dark Dozen anthology that explores themes of horror focused on being trapped in an unspeakable situation.

Uncomfortably Dark presents Dark Disasters-2023 Dark Dozen anthology that explores horrific situations unfolding during natural disasters.

Uncomfortably Dark presents Full Throttle-2025 Dark Dozen Anthology that is a full-blown extreme horror anthology dedicated to survivors of sexual violence.

This anthology contains no scenes of sexual violence.

The Generator-quad collaboration anthology featuring Candace Nola, Eric Butler, M Ennenbach, and Nikolas P. Robinson.

Dark Disturbances- 2024 Uncomfortably Dark
Author Sampler Anthology.

<u>NOVELS & COLLECTIONS</u>

EPISODES OF VIOLENCE by David Bernstein

DREAMWHISPERS by M Ennenbach

CREMATED REMAINS by M Ennenbach

CUCKOO by M Ennenbach

WHERE THE DEAD DON'T DIE by Ronald J.
Murray

IN ALL THE WAYS, A DROWNING by Ronald J.
Murray

OLD TOO SOON by Brian Bowyer

BLACKOUT: MICROPOETRY by Brian Bowyer

INNOCENCE ENDS by Nikolas P. Robinson

HAVE A BLAST by Nikolas P. Robinson

COME OUT & PLAY by Patrick Tumblety

ROADS TO RUIN by Brian Bowyer

SUBJECT A by M Ennenbach

OIOS LYKOS by M Ennenbach

STORYSLAVE by Brian Bowyer

VERUM MALUM by Michael R. Collins

PENNYROYAL TEA by Aaron LeBold

THE SHERIFF OF SALEM by Aaron LeBold

GENOCIDE by Aaron LeBold

QUARANTINE by Aaron LeBold

**Order signed copies and limited-edition
hardcovers from the shop:
https://www.uncomfortablydark.com/shop
Join our Patreon for free books, merch, and more!**
https://www.patreon.com/user/membership?u=12231
330&view_as=patron